THE FALCON'S MALTESER

A Diamond Brothers Mystery

ANTHONY HOROWITZ

PUFFIN BOOKS

For
Dursley McLinden
5/29/65–8/7/95
who played Tim Diamond in the film and in the TV series

PUFFIN BOOKS
Published by Penguin Group
Penguin Young Readers Group,
345 Hudson Street, New York, New York 10014, U.S.A.
Penguin Books Ltd, 80 Strand, London WC2R ORL, England
Penguin Books Australia Ltd, 250 Camberwell Road, Camberwell, Victoria 3124, Australia
Penguin Books Canada Ltd, 10 Alcorn Avenue, Toronto, Ontario, Canada M4V 3B2
Penguin Group (NZ) cnr Airborne and Rosedale Roads, Albany, Auckland 1310, New Zealand

Published in Great Britain by Walker Books Ltd, 1995
Published simultaneously in the United States of America by Philomel Books
and Puffin Books, divisions of Penguin Young Readers Group, 2004

1 3 5 7 9 10 8 6 4 2

Puffin Books ISBN 0-14-240219-2

This book refers to a famous product, MALTESERS chocolates, manufactured by Mars UK
Limited. Mr. Horowitz wishes to make it clear that this book is solely his invention and
that Mars UK Limited in no way initiated, sponsored, or approved the work.

Printed in the United States of America

BUSTED!

Johnny Naples was lying on the bed. He wasn't dead yet, but the big red splotch on his shirt told me that his time was running out about as quickly as his blood. I went over to the window and looked outside. But I was too late. Whoever had climbed out had jumped the short distance to the overpass and run for it. Maybe they'd had a car waiting for them. Anyway, they were gone.

The dwarf groaned and I looked back again. Johnny opened his mouth and tried to speak.

"The falcon . . ." he said. Then a nasty, bubbling sound.

Then: "The sun . . ." And that was it. His eyes closed. The mouth stayed open.

D for "dwarf." *D* for "dead."

Herbert had picked something up off the carpet.

"Nick . . ." he began.

It was a gun. And it was still smoking.

And he was still standing there, holding it, when the door crashed open. The man who had been drunk outside the Hotel Splendide was standing there and he had a gun, too. The Alsatian was with him, growling softly.

There were two more people behind him.

"Police!" he shouted.

Herbert fainted.

The man swung around to cover him. "You're under arrest," he said.

BOOKS BY ANTHONY HOROWITZ

CONTENTS

THE PACKAGE

There's not much call for private detectives in Fulham.

The day it all started was a bad one. Business was so slack it was falling down all around us. The gas had been disconnected that morning, one of the coldest mornings for twenty years, and it could only be a matter of time before the electricity followed. We'd run out of food and the people in the supermarket downstairs had all fallen down laughing when I suggested credit. We had just $2.37 and about three teaspoons of instant coffee to last us the weekend. The wallpaper was peeling, the carpets were fraying, and the curtains . . . well, whichever way you looked at it, it was curtains for us. Even the cockroaches were walking out.

I was just wondering whether the time hadn't finally come to do something constructive—like packing my bags and going back to Mum—when the door opened and the dwarf walked in.

Okay—maybe you're not supposed to call them dwarfs these days. Vertically challenged . . . that's what it says in the book. But not this book. The truth is, this guy was as challenged as they come. I was only thirteen but already I had six inches on him, and the way he looked at me with cold, unforgiving eyes—he knew it and wasn't going to forget it.

He was in his midforties, I guessed. It was hard to say with someone that size. A short, dark stranger with brown eyes and a snub nose. He was wearing a three-piece suit, only the pieces all belonged to different suits like he'd gotten dressed in a hurry. His socks didn't match either. A neat mustache crowned his upper lip and his black hair was slicked back with oil. A spotted bow tie and a flashy gold ring completed the picture. It was a weird picture.

"Do come in, Mr. . . ." my brother began.

"Naples," the dwarf, who already was in, said. His name might have come out of Italy, but he spoke with a South American accent. "Johnny Naples. You are Tim Diamond?"

"That's me," my brother lied. His real name was Herbert Timothy Simple, but he called himself Tim Diamond. He thought it suited his image. "And what can I do for you, Mr. Venice?"

"Naples," the dwarf corrected him. He climbed onto a chair and sat down opposite my brother. His nose just reached the level of the desk. Herbert slid a paperweight out of the way to give his new client a clear view. The dwarf was about to speak when he paused and the nose turned toward me. "Who is he?" he demanded, the two hs scratching at the back of his throat.

"Him?" Herbert smiled. "He's just my kid brother. Don't worry about him, Mr. Navels. Just tell me how I can help you."

Naples laid a carefully manicured hand on the desk. His

initials—JN—were cut into a gleaming ring. There was so much gold around that third finger he could have added his name and address, too. "I want to deposit something with you," he said.

"Deposit?" Herbert repeated quite unnecessarily. The dwarf might have had a thick accent, but it certainly wasn't as thick as my brother. "You mean . . . like in a bank?" he continued, brilliantly.

The dwarf raised his eyes to the ceiling, took in the crack in the plaster, and then, with a sigh, lowered them onto Herbert. "I want to leave a package with you," he said briskly. "It's important you look after it. But you must not open it. Just keep it here and keep it safe."

"For how long?"

Now the dwarf's eyes darted across to the window. He swallowed hard and loosened his bow tie. I could see that he was scared of something or somebody in the street outside. Either that or he had a fear of storm windows.

"I don't know," he replied. "About a week maybe. I'll come back and collect it . . . when I can. You give it to nobody else except for me. You understand?"

Naples pulled out a packet of Turkish cigarettes and lit one. The smoke curled upward, a lurid blue in the chill morning air. My brother flicked a piece of chewing gum toward his mouth. It missed and disappeared over his shoulder.

"What's in the package?" he asked.

"That's my business," the dwarf said.

"Okay. Let's talk about my business, then." Herbert treated his client to one of his "don't mess with me" smiles. It made him look about as menacing as a cow with a stomachache. "I'm not cheap," he went on. "If you want a cheap private eye, try looking in the cemetery. You want me to look after your package? It'll cost you."

The dwarf reached into his jacket pocket and pulled out the first good thing I'd seen that week: fifty portraits of Alexander Hamilton, each one printed in green. In other words, a bundle of ten-dollar bills, brand-new and crisp. "There's five hundred dollars here," he said.

"Five hundred?" Herbert squeaked.

"There will be another five hundred when I return and pick up the package. I take it that is sufficient?"

My brother nodded his head, an insane grin on his face. Put him in the back of a car and who'd need a bobbing-head doll?

"Good." The dwarf stubbed out his half-smoked cigarette and slid off the chair. Then he removed a plain brown envelope from another pocket. It was quite thick with something vaguely rectangular bulging in the center. It rattled faintly as he put it on the desk. "Here is the package," he said. "Once again, look after it, Mr. Diamond. With your life. And whatever you do, don't open it."

"You can trust me, Mr. Nipples," my brother muttered. "Your package is in safe hands." He waved one of the safe hands to illustrate the point, sending a mug of coffee flying.

"What happens if I need to get in touch with you?" he asked as an afterthought.

"You don't," Naples snapped. "I get in touch with you."

"Well, there's no need to be touchy," Herbert said.

It was then that a car in the street backfired. The dwarf seemed to evaporate. One moment he was standing beside the desk. The next he was crouching beneath it, one hand inside his jacket. And somehow I knew that his finger wasn't wrapped round another bundle of money. For about thirty seconds nobody moved. Then Naples slid across to the window, standing to one side so that he could look out without being seen. He had to stand on tiptoe to do it, his hands perched on the sill, the side of his face pressed against the glass. When he turned around, he left a damp circle on the window. Hair oil and sweat.

"I'll see you again in a week," he said. He made for the door as fast as his legs could carry him. With his legs, that wasn't too fast. "Look after that package with your life, Mr. Diamond," he repeated. "And I mean . . . your life."

And then he was gone.

My brother was jubilant. "Five hundred bucks just for looking after an envelope," he crowed. "This is my lucky day. This is the best thing that's happened to me this year." He glanced at the package. "I wonder what's in it?" he murmured. "Still, that shouldn't worry us. As far as we're concerned, there's no problem."

That's what Herbert thought. But right from the start I

wasn't so sure. I mean, five hundred dollars is five hundred dollars, and when you're throwing that sort of money around, there's got to be a good reason. And I remembered the dwarf's face when the car backfired. He may have been a small guy, but he seemed to be expecting big trouble.

Just how big I was to find out soon enough.

TIM DIAMOND INC.

The five hundred dollars lasted about half a day. But it was a good half day.

It began with a blowout at a café round the corner. Double eggs, double sausage, double fries, and fried bread but no beans. We'd been living on beans for the best part of a week. It had gotten so bad I'd been having nightmares about giant Heinz cans chasing me down the High Street.

After that, Herbert put an ad in the local paper for a cleaning lady. That was crazy, really. There was no way we could afford one—but on the other hand, if you'd seen the state of our place, maybe you'd have understood. Dust everywhere, dirty plates piled high in the sink, and old socks sprawled across the carpet from the bedroom to the front door as if they were trying to get to the Laundromat under their own steam. Then we took a bus into the West End. Herbert bought me a new jacket for the next term at school and bought himself some new thermal underwear and a hot-water bottle. That left just about enough money to get two tickets for a film. We went to see *101 Dalmations*. Herbert cried all the way through. He even cried in the coming attractions. That's what sort of guy he is.

I suppose it was pretty strange, the two of us living

together the way we did. It had all happened about two years back when my parents suddenly decided to emigrate to Australia. Herbert was twenty-three then. I'd just turned eleven.

We were living in a comfortable house in a nice part of London. I still remember the address: 1 Wiernotta Mews. My dad worked as a door-to-door salesman. Doors was what he sold; fancy French sliding doors and traditional English doors, pure mahogany, made in Korea. He really loved doors. Ours was the only house in the street with seventeen ways in. As for my mum, she had a part-time job in a pet shop. It was after she got bitten by a rabid parrot that they decided to emigrate. I wasn't exactly wild about the idea, but of course nobody asked me. You know how some parents think they own their kids? Well, I couldn't even sneeze without written permission signed in duplicate.

Neither Herbert nor I really got on with our parents. That was one thing we had in common. Oh yeah . . . and we didn't get on with each other. That was the second thing. He'd just joined the police force (this was one week before the Hendon Police Training Center burned down) and could more or less look after himself, but of course I had as much independence as the coffee table.

"You'll love Australia," my dad said. "It's got kangaroos."

"And boomerangs," my mum added.

"And wonderful, maple-wood doors . . ."

"And koalas."

"I'm not going!" I said.

"You are!" they screamed.

So much for reasoned argument.

I got as far as Heathrow Airport. But just as the plane to Sydney was about to take off, I slipped out the back door and managed to find my way out of the airport. Then I hightailed it back to Fulham. I'm told my mum had hysterics about thirty-five thousand feet above Bangkok. But by then it was too late.

Now, by this time, Herbert had finished with the police force, or to put it more accurately, the police force had finished with Herbert. He'd finally gotten fired for giving someone directions to a bank. I suppose it wasn't his fault that the someone had robbed it, but he really shouldn't have held the door for the guy as he came out. But in the meantime, he'd managed to save up some money and had rented this run-down apartment in the Fulham Road, above a supermarket, planning to set himself up as a private detective. That's what it said on the door:

TIM DIAMOND INC.
PRIVATE DETECTIVE

Inside, you went up a staircase to a glass-fronted door, which in turn led into his office, a long, narrow room with four windows looking out into the street. A second door led off from here into the kitchen. The staircase continued up to a second floor, where we both had a bedroom and shared a bathroom. The apartment had been made available to Herbert at a bargain-basement price, probably because the whole place was so rickety it was threatening to collapse into the basement at any time. The stairs wobbled when you went up and the bath wobbled when you turned on the taps. We never saw the landlord. I think he was afraid to come near the place.

Dark-haired and blue-eyed, Herbert was quite handsome—at least from the opposite side of the street on a foggy day. But what God had given him in looks, He had taken away in brains. There might have been worse private detectives than Tim Diamond. But somehow I doubt it.

I'll give you an example. His first job was to find some rich lady's pedigree Siamese cat. He managed to run it over on the way to see her. The second job was a divorce case—which you may think is run-of-the-mill until I tell you that the clients were perfectly happily married until he came along.

There hadn't been a third case.

Anyway, Herbert was not overjoyed to see me that day when I turned up from Heathrow carrying a suitcase that held exactly nothing, but where else could I go? We argued. I told him it was a fait accompli. We argued some more. I told him what a fait accompli was. In the end he let me stay.

Mind you, I often wondered if I'd made the right decision. For a start, when I say I like a square meal a day I don't mean a sawed-off shredded wheat, and it's no fun starting the winter term in clothes you grew out of the summer before, with more holes in your socks than a Swiss cheese. We could never afford anything. Her Majesty's government helped Herbert out a little, which is a fancy way of saying that he got welfare, and my parents sent the occasional check for my upkeep, but even so, Herbert never managed to make ends meet. I tried to persuade him to get himself a sensible job—anything other than private detection—but it was hopeless. As hopeless as Herbert himself.

Anyway, after the movie, we got back to the flat around eleven and were making our way up the stairs past the office when Herbert stopped. "Wait a minute, Nick," he said. "Did you leave the door open?"

"No," I said.

"That's strange . . ."

He was right. The door of the office was open, the moonlight pouring out of the crack like someone had spilled a can of silver paint. We made our way back downstairs and went in. I turned on the light.

"Oh dear," my brother said. "I think we've had visitors."

That was the understatement of the year. A stampede of wild bulls would have left the place in better order. The desk had been torn open, the carpets torn up, the bookshelves torn apart, and the curtains torn down. The old filing cabinet would have fit into so many matchboxes. Even the telephone had been demolished, its various parts scattered around the room. Whoever had been there, they'd done a thorough job. If we'd been invited to a wedding, we could have taken the office along for confetti.

"Oh dear," Herbert repeated. He stepped into the rubble

and picked up what was now a very dead cactus. A moment later, he dropped it, his lower jaw falling at about the same speed. "My God!" he shrieked. "The envelope!"

He stumbled over to the remains of his desk and searched in the rubble of the top drawer. "I put it here," he said. He fumbled about on the floor. "It's gone!" he moaned at last. He got back to his feet, clenching and unclenching his fists. "The first job I've had in six months and now I've gone and lost it. You know what this means, don't you? It means we won't get the other five hundred dollars. I'll probably have to pay back the five hundred we've already spent. What a disaster! What a catastrophe! I don't know why I bother, really I don't. It's just not fair!" He gave the desk a great thump with his boot. It groaned and collapsed in a small heap.

Then he looked at me. "Well, don't just stand there," he snapped.

"What am I supposed to do?" I asked.

"Well . . . say something."

"All right," I said. "I didn't think it was a very good idea to leave the package in your desk . . ."

"It's a fat lot of good telling me now," Herbert whined. It looked as though he was going to cry.

"I didn't think it was a good idea," I continued, "so I took it with me." I pulled the envelope out of my jacket pocket, where it had been resting all evening.

My brother seized it and gave it a big wet kiss. He didn't even thank me.

THE FAT MAN

We didn't get much sleep that night. First we had to make our beds—and I'm not just talking sheets and blankets. Whoever had wrecked our office had done the same for the rest of the apartment. It took about forty nails and two tubes of Super Glue before the beds were even recognizable, and then I found that Herbert had managed to stick himself to the door handle and had to spend another hour prying him free with a kitchen knife. By then it was morning and I was too tired to sleep. Herbert sent me out for a loaf of bread while he put on the teakettle. At least they hadn't dismantled the kettle.

There were three letters on the doormat and I brought them up with the bread. One was a bill. One was postmarked Sydney, Australia. And the third had been delivered by hand. Herbert filed the bill under *W* for "wastepaper basket" while I opened the Australian letter.

Darling Herbert and Nicky [it read],

Just a quick note as Daddy and I are about to go to a barbecue. They have lots of barbecues in Australia. The weather's lovely. The sun never stops shining—even when it's raining. You really ought to come out here.

I hope you are well. We miss you both very, very much.

Have you solved any crimes yet? It must be very cold in England, so make sure you bundle up well with a vest. I know they tickle, but pneumonia is no laughing matter. I'm enclosing a little check so you can go to Marks & Spencer.

Must go now. Daddy's at the door. He's just bought a new one.

I'll write again soon.

Love, Mumsy

It was written on the back of a postcard showing a picture of the Sydney Opera House. There was a check attached with a paper clip: seventy-five dollars. It wasn't a fortune, but at least it would pay for a few more tubes of Super Glue. Herbert pocketed the check. I kept the card.

The third letter was the most interesting. It was typed on a single sheet of paper with no address at the top. It was a big sheet of paper, but it was a short letter.

```
DIAMOND—
TRAFALGAR SQUARE. 1:00 P.M. BE THERE.
The Fat Man.
```

"Who the hell is the Fat Man?" I asked.

"The Fat Man . . ." Herbert muttered. His face had gone a sort of cheesy white and his mouth was hanging open. The last time I had seen him look like that had been when he found a spider in the bath.

"Who is he?"

Herbert was tugging at the letter. It tore in half. "The Fat Man is about the biggest criminal in England," he croaked.

"You mean . . . the fattest?"

"No. The biggest. He's involved in everything. Burglary, armed robbery, fraud, arson, armed burglary . . . You name it, he's behind it."

"How do you know?" I asked.

"From when I was a policeman," Herbert explained. "Every crook has a file at New Scotland Yard. But the Fat Man has a whole library. He's clever. Nobody's ever been able to arrest him. Not once. A traffic cop once gave him a parking ticket. They found her a week later, embedded in concrete, part of the M6 highway. Nobody tangles with the Fat Man. He's death."

Herbert pressed the two halves of the letter together as if he could magically restore them. Personally, I was more puzzled than afraid. Okay—so there was this master criminal called the Fat Man. But what could he want with a loser like Herbert? Obviously it had to be something to do with the dwarf's mysterious package. Had the Fat Man been responsible for the destruction of the apartment? It seemed likely, and yet at the same time I doubted it. You don't tear someone's place apart and then casually invite them to meet you in Trafalgar Square. One or the other—but not both. On the other hand, if he hadn't done it, who had?

"What are we going to do?" I asked.

"Do?" Herbert looked at me as though I were mad.

"We're going! When the Fat Man invites you to jump in front of a subway train, you don't argue. You just do it. And you're grateful he wasn't in a bad mood!"

So later that morning we took the number 14 bus into the West End. This time I left the package—carefully hidden—back at the flat. It had been ransacked once and I figured that nobody would think of looking for it there a second time.

"How will we recognize the Fat Man?" I asked.

"I've seen mug shots," Herbert said.

"You mean—you even had pictures of him on your mugs?"

Herbert didn't laugh. You could have tickled the soles of his feet with an ostrich feather and he wouldn't have laughed. He was so scared, he could barely talk. *And* he ate the bus tickets.

The bus dropped us in Piccadilly Circus and we walked across to Trafalgar Square. It was another cold day with a bite in the air that bit all the way through. The tourist season had ended weeks before, but there were still a few of them around, taking photographs of one another against the gray December sky. The Christmas decorations had gone up in Regent Street—it seemed that they'd been up since July—and the stores were wrapped in tinsel and holly. Somewhere, a Salvation Army band was playing "Away in a Manger." I felt a funeral march would have been more appropriate.

Trafalgar Square is a big place and the Fat Man hadn't been too specific about the meeting point, so we positioned ourselves right in the middle, under Nelson's Column. There were a few tourists feeding the pigeons. I felt sorry for them. Who'd be a pigeon in London . . . or for that matter a tourist? I had a candy bar, so I pulled out a couple of peanuts and fed them myself. I ate the rest of it. It was already ten minutes to one and in all the excitement I'd missed out on breakfast. Taxis, buses, cars, and trucks rumbled all around us, streaming down to the Houses of Parliament and across to Buckingham Palace. I leaned against a lion, looking out for anyone with a fifty-inch waist. A pigeon landed on my shoulder and I gave it another peanut.

Big Ben struck one. According to my watch, it was five minutes fast.

"There he is," Herbert said.

I didn't see him at first. At least, I saw him but I didn't see him. A pink Rolls-Royce had pulled up at the curb, ignoring the blasts of the cars trapped behind it. A chauffeur got out, strolled round to the back, and opened the door for one of the thinnest men I had ever seen. He was so thin that, as he moved toward us, he was like a living skeleton. His clothes—an expensive Italian suit and fur-lined coat—hung off him like they were trying to get away. Even his rings were too big for his pencil fingers. As he walked, he kept adjusting them to stop them from sliding off.

I looked from him to Herbert and back again. "That's the Fat Man?" I asked.

Herbert nodded. "He's lost weight."

He reached us and stopped, swaying slightly as if the wind was going to blow him away. Close up, he was even more peculiar than far away. Hollow cheeks, hollow eyes, hollow gut. The man was a drum with skin stretched so tight over bones you could probably see right through him when the light was behind him.

"Mr. Diamond?" he said.

"Yes," Herbert admitted.

"I'm the Fat Man."

There was a long silence. Herbert was too afraid to talk, but I don't like long silences. They make me nervous. "You don't look fat to me," I said.

The Fat Man chuckled unpleasantly. Even his laughter was hollow. "Who are you?" he demanded.

"Nick Diamond," I told him, adopting my brother's name. "I'm his kid brother."

"Well, my dear boy, might I suggest that you keep your young mouth closed? I have business with your brother."

I kept my young mouth closed. The Fat Man didn't bother me, but I was interested to know what his business was. Meanwhile, the chauffeur had followed him from the Rolls, carrying a folding chair and a tub of corn. The chauffeur was wearing glasses that were so dark they didn't show his eyes, but rather two reflections of yourself. He unfolded the chair and handed his master the corn.

"Thank you, Lawrence," the Fat Man said. "You can wait in the car."

The chauffeur grunted and walked away. The Fat Man sat down, then dug a hand into the tub and threw a spray of kernels across the concrete. The pigeons came at us in a rush. He smiled briefly.

"You look well," Herbert muttered.

"Thank you . . . Timothy, if I may so call you." The Fat Man was genuinely pleased. "My doctor advised me to lose weight." He shrugged. "One must bow to the voice of reason—although some might say I have taken it a touch far. For the past year I have eaten nothing but yogurt and have shed two hundred and ninety-five pounds. I have, however, retained my old nickname for professional purposes." The hand dug again, scattering more corn for the pigeons. "On the subject of which," the Fat Man continued, "I will be brief. You were visited yesterday by an old friend of mine. A small friend. I am led to understand that he might have entrusted you with something, something that I want. Something that I'm willing to pay for."

Herbert said nothing, so I chipped in. "How much?"

The Fat Man smiled at me a second time. He had dreadful teeth. In fact he was pretty dreadful all over.

"You seem a bright lad," he said. "I'm sure the nurses will just adore you in the emergency room."

I shrugged. "We don't have it," I said.

"You don't?" His eyebrows lifted themselves toward his bald head. At the same time, he fed the pigeons.

"Our place was turned over last night," I explained.

"Perhaps you know about that already. Whoever did it took what you're looking for."

"That's right!" Herbert agreed. "That's what happened."

The Fat Man looked at us suspiciously. He was pretty sure that we were lying. But he couldn't be certain. A pigeon landed on his head with a flutter of gray feathers. He punched it off, then threw corn at it. At last he spoke. "Taken?" he murmured.

"Absolutely," Herbert said. "When we got back from the movies, it wasn't there. Otherwise we'd love to give it to you. Really we would."

I groaned silently. We'd have been all right if only Herbert had kept his mouth shut. But he couldn't have convinced a six-year-old and I could tell that the Fat Man had seen right through him. I glanced nervously at the chauffeur, who was watching us from the front seat of the Rolls. Was he armed? Almost certainly. But would he try anything in the middle of Trafalgar Square?

"Very well," the Fat Man said, and suddenly his voice was colder than the winter wind. "We shall play the game your way, my friends. If you want to find out what the bottom of the Thames looks like on a December night, that's your affair." He stood up and now his face was ugly. Actually, it had been ugly before he had even started, but now it was even worse. "I want the key," he growled. "Perhaps, soon, you will find it again. Should such a happy event take place, I'm confident you won't be foolish enough to keep it from me." He dipped two fingers into his top pocket. When he pulled them out again, he was holding a card, which he gave to Herbert.

"My number," he went on. "I am a patient man, Timothy. I can wait all of forty-eight hours. But if I haven't heard from you in two days, I think you may wake up to find that something very unpleasant has happened to you. Like you no longer have any feet."

"Why do you want this . . . key so badly?" I demanded.

The Fat Man didn't answer me. We'd hit it off—him and me. The way he was looking at my head, I figured he'd like to hit that off, too. But then his eyes wandered. He jerked his hand, sending the rest of the corn flying. The pigeons were all around him, bowing their heads at his feet.

"I hate pigeons," he said in a faraway voice. "Flying rats! London is infested with them. I hate the noise they make, day and night, the filth that they leave behind them. The government ought to make them illegal. And yet they're encouraged! It makes me sick to think of them scuttling across the pavements, infesting the trees, carrying their germs and diseases—"

"So why do you feed them?" I shouldn't have asked, but I had to know.

The Fat Man laughed briefly, mirthlessly. Then he spun the empty carton in my direction. "Poisoned corn," he said.

He walked back to the car and got in. A few feet away, a pigeon suddenly gurgled and keeled over on its side. A moment later, two more joined it, their feet sticking up in the air.

By the time the Rolls-Royce had reached the corner of Trafalgar Square and turned off toward Hyde Park, we were surrounded by corpses.

"Do you think he's trying to tell us something?" I said.

Herbert didn't answer. He wasn't looking much better
than the pigeons.

OPENING TIME

Before the bus had even arrived to take us back to Fulham, we both knew that we were going to have to open the dwarf's package. We hadn't had it twenty-four hours, but already our apartment had been ransacked and we'd attracted the poisonous attention of the biggest crook in the country. Okay— so Johnny Naples had paid us five hundred dollars. He made us promise not to open the envelope. But promises are easily broken. So are necks. I knew which I wanted to see get broken first.

There was a woman waiting at the door when the bus dropped us off. What with the dwarf and the Fat Man, I figured I'd already seen enough weird people for one day, but it seemed that today, like buses and musketeers, they were coming in threes.

She was an old woman with gray, curling hair that stuck out like someone had just electrocuted her. Her lipstick, a vivid shade of crimson, was pretty electrifying, too. Her skin was a mass of wrinkles, hanging on her like an old coat. An old coat hung on her, too, a sort of seaweed green color with artificial fur trimmings. She had a hat like a tea cozy on her head and a bulging carpetbag in her hand. Although this was a main street in the middle of Fulham, her feet were lost in blue fluffy slippers.

We assumed that she had drifted out of the local lunatic asylum and let ourselves into the apartment, ignoring her. It was only when we got into the office and found her still behind us that we realized that she had been waiting to see us. Now she took one look at the wreckage and whistled, smacking her lips together afterward as if she'd just swallowed a gumball.

"Cor blimey!" she exclaimed. "Luv-a-duck! What a blooming mess!"

"Who are you?" Herbert demanded.

"Charlady," she replied. She gave us a big, crimson smile. "I saw your ad in the newspaper."

With everything that had happened, we'd quite forgotten about our advertisement for a cleaning lady. But here a cleaning lady was.

"Oh yes," Herbert muttered. "What's your name?"

"Charlady."

"Yes. I know." He frowned. I shrugged. Maybe she didn't understand English. Maybe somebody had dropped her when she was a baby. Herbert tried again, more slowly. "What—is—your—name?"

"Charlady!" she said for a third time. "Betty Charlady. That's my name. But you can call me Betty."

Without waiting for an invitation, she stepped farther into the room, waving a feather duster that she had produced out of nowhere, like a demented magician. Herbert and I looked at each other as she brushed it lightly across the remains of a shelf. The shelf fell off the wall. The cleaning lady scowled. "Crikey!" she said. "Wot a disaster. You don't need a blooming cleaner 'ere, luv. You need a master carpenter!"

"Wait a minute—" Herbert began.

"Don't you worry!" she interrupted. The duster had vanished and now she was holding a hammer. "It won't take me a minute. I'll soon 'ave this place looking like new."

I didn't doubt her. The carpetbag was so bulky it could have had a box of nails, a screwdriver, and even a stepladder concealed in it, too. But Herbert had managed to hold her down long enough to get her attention.

"I . . . we . . . well . . ." He'd gotten her attention, but he didn't know what to do with it.

"How much do you charge?" I asked.

"Twenny a day," she chirped, then, seeing the look of dismay on our faces: "Well . . . a tenner for you. You look nice-enough lads to me. And a private detective, too! I love detective stories. Ten dollars a day and I'll bring me own tea bags. What do you say?"

I could see Herbert was about to send her on her way, so I moved quickly. We'd spent the five hundred dollars, but we still had the check that Mum had sent us that morning. If Betty Charlady could rebuild the flat and then clean it, too— and all for ten dollars a day—it seemed too good a bargain to miss.

"You can start on Monday," I said.

"Nick . . ." Herbert protested.

"Do you really want to live in this?" I asked, pointing at the room.

"'E's right," Betty chipped in. "'E's a lovely boy, ineee! Wot is 'e? Your bruvver?" Herbert nodded. "'E's a real knockout." She curtsied at me. "A proper little gentleman. Monday, you say? Well, I'd still like to start now if it's all the same with you. Strike while the iron is 'ot, as I always say."

"The iron's in about a hundred pieces," I said. "Along with the ironing board."

It wasn't that funny, but she threw back her head and laughed like a drain. You know the sort of gurgling sound that water makes when you take the plug out of the bath? Well, that was the sort of drain she laughed like.

"We're rather busy now," Herbert said. I could see he was itching to get at that package. "Can you come back on Monday?"

"I'll be 'ere," Betty promised. "Nine o'clock on the dot."

"Make it ten."

"Ten o'clock, then." She curtsied again. "Wot a little darling—eh?" She winked. "Ten o'clock. Blimey!" Then she went.

We waited until we heard the outer door close before we retrieved the package. There was a loose floorboard in the office—in fact there were more loose floorboards than sound ones—and I'd hidden it underneath, covering it with a layer of dust. Herbert took the envelope and I shook it. Once again it rattled. He was about to open it, but then he froze.

"It could be a bomb," he whispered.

"A bomb?" I repeated. "Why should Naples have left us a bomb?"

"Well . . ."

"And who would search the place for a bomb?"

Herbert nodded. "That's right," he said. "You're right, Nick. Of course it isn't a bomb. I mean, there's no way it could be a bomb." He laughed. "I mean, who could possibly think . . ." He thrust it into my hands. "You open it."

With a little smile, he retreated into the far corner of the room, leaving the package with me. I shook it again. The Fat Man had said he wanted "the key." Whatever the package contained, it certainly wasn't a key. It sounded more like marbles— a lot of marbles in a cardboard container. I could feel the lid bending under my fingers. Herbert was watching me like a hawk. No. He was more like a rabbit. I tossed the package into the air and caught it. He blinked and shivered.

A bomb? Of course not.

But it could still be booby-trapped.

I stuck my thumb under the flap and slid it slowly sideways, trying to feel for a concealed wire or thread. Johnny Naples hadn't used a lot of spit when he stuck it down. Perhaps his tongue had been as dry as mine was now. The flap came loose without tearing. I caught a flash of red inside. There was a box of some sort. I tilted the package.

The box slid out onto the floor. Herbert dived for cover. But there was no bang.

And then we were both looking down, wondering if we'd gone crazy. Or perhaps we were about to go crazy. Certainly someone, somewhere, had to be crazy.

There was only one thing in the dwarf's package.

It was a box of candy.

D FOR "DWARF"

Maltesers. That's what it said on the box. You can buy them just about anywhere in the world even if the name isn't always the same. Maltesers are those chocolate malt balls that crunch when you eat them. Personally, I've never been that keen on eating them at all. I've got better things to spend my pocket money on. New pockets, for example. The old ones are full of holes.

The question was, why had Johnny Naples paid out five hundred dollars to have us look after a box of candy? Why had someone gone to so much trouble—wrecking the apartment—to get his hands on them? And how had the Fat Man gotten mixed up in all this? Chocolates were the last things he needed—he was on a diet. It just didn't make sense.

We'd opened up the box. In for a penny, in for a pound (or 5.15 ounces, to be exact). The contents certainly looked like ordinary Maltesers. They smelled ordinary. And they tasted ordinary. Herbert had some sort of idea that they might be chocolate-covered diamonds or something. It was only after I'd eaten half a dozen of them that he changed his mind and suggested that they might contain some sort of newfangled poison. If looks could kill, I'd have buried my brother.

"What we've got to do," Herbert said, "is find Naples."

For Herbert that was a pretty brilliant piece of deduction. The Fat Man had given us two days to get back to him. Johnny Naples had said he'd return in about a week. That left five days in which all sorts of unpleasant things could happen. The only trouble was, Naples hadn't told us where we could reach him. We had no address, no telephone number.

Herbert echoed my thoughts. "I wonder how we could get hold of him?" he asked.

"We could try the Yellow Pages," I suggested. "*V* for 'vertically challenged'?"

"Yes!"

I groaned as he reached for the telephone book. "I was only joking," I said.

"Were you? Of course you were!" Herbert dropped the book and gazed out of the window.

Meanwhile, I was fingering the envelope. The Maltesers hadn't told us anything, but looking underneath the flap, I found a small white label. The dwarf, in a hurry to seal the package, must have missed it. "Look at this," I said.

Herbert took the envelope. "It's an envelope," he said.

"Yes. But look at the label."

Herbert found it and held it up to the light. "Hammett's," he read. "Eighteen cents." He frowned. "That's cheap for a box of Maltesers."

I shook my head. "That's the price of the envelope, not the candy," I explained. "Look—the price is handwritten, but the name is printed. Hammett's . . . that must be the stationer's or newsstand where he bought the envelope to put the Maltesers in."

"That's terrific!" Herbert exclaimed. "That's great, Nick." He paused. "But how does it help us?"

"If the dwarf wanted to buy an envelope, he probably bought it fairly near wherever he's staying," I said. "So all we have to do is find out how many Hammett's shops there are in London, visit them all, and ask them if they remember selling an envelope to Naples."

Herbert sighed. "They probably sell hundreds of envelopes," he said. "And they must have thousands of customers."

"Yeah. But how many of their customers are dwarfs?"

"That's true." He considered. "So how do we find Hammett's?"

"We look in the Yellow Pages."

Herbert snatched up the book again. Then he turned and looked at me disdainfully. "That was my idea in the first place," he said.

I didn't argue. Arguing with someone like Herbert is a bit like hitting yourself with a brick.

As it turned out, there were six Hammett's in London.

We found them under the section headed *Newsstands and News Vendors.* There were three south of the river, one in Notting Hill Gate, one in Kensington, and one in Hammersmith.

By now it was too late to visit them all, so we decided to take the three in the south first and pick up some secondhand furniture from a friend with a shop near Clapham Common at the same time. It took us a couple of hours and a lot of wasted shoe leather, but at least that evening we were able to sit down again.

The next day was a Saturday. We left the flat for a second time, but struck out in Kensington and Hammersmith. That just left Notting Hill Gate. The last Hammett's was a run-down place on the Portobello Road in the middle of a famous antiques and bric-a-brac market. The sun was shining and the market was busy with young couples shelling out for Victorian brass towel holders and Edwardian stripped-pine blanket boxes. The air was thick with the smell of french fries and overcooked kebabs. Outside the shop there was an old boy selling genuine antique license plates. Doubtless they had fallen off a genuine antique truck.

The shop was small and dark. That seemed to be the trademark of the entire Hammett's chain. You probably know the sort of place: candy and chocolates on one side, newspapers and magazines on the other, with the dirty stuff on the top shelf. Herbert made straight for it, thumbing through a copy of *Playboy,* "looking for clues," as he put it. Meanwhile, I took a quick look at the stationery and odds-and-ends section. This was the first branch we'd visited that actually stocked the right-size envelopes. I examined a price label. The handwriting was the same.

There was only one man behind the counter. He was about forty, a cigarette dangling out of the corner of his mouth, his skin the unhealthy shade of white that comes from sitting in a dingy newsstand all day smoking. While Herbert continued his own private investigation, I took the envelope and went over to him.

"Excuse me," I said. "I know this is going to sound crazy, but do you remember selling one of these envelopes to a dwarf?"

The man looked past me at Herbert. "Are you going to buy that?" he barked. Herbert pushed the magazine away from him and blushed. Then he came over and joined us. "Now, what do you want, son?" the newsagent asked.

"My brother's a private detective," I explained. "We're trying to find a dwarf . . . greasy hair, suntan. We think he bought an envelope here a couple of days ago."

"Yeah . . . I remember that." The newsagent nodded. "A short guy . . ."

"Most dwarfs are," I muttered.

"Came in here . . . last Thursday."

It had been Thursday when Johnny Naples came to see us. I was beginning to get excited, but then Herbert had to pipe up. "Diamond's the name," he said. "Tim Diamond."

"He didn't tell me his name," the newsagent said.

"No. I'm telling you my name."

The newsagent frowned at me. "Is he all right?" he asked.

"Sure." I scowled at Herbert. "Look—this is important.

Did the dwarf buy anything else here? Like some Maltesers, for example."

I could see that the man was beginning to have second thoughts about the state of my own sanity, but he knew I was serious. He considered for a minute. "He didn't buy any candy," he said. "But . . . now I remember. He had a box of Maltesers with him when he came in. I saw him put them in the envelope. What else did he buy? There was something . . ." He snapped his fingers. "It was a pair of scissors." Now it all came back. "He was in a hurry. Nervous sort. Kept on looking out into the street. Like he was being followed or something. He bought an envelope and a pair of scissors. Then he went."

"We need to find him," I said.

"Is he in some sort of trouble?" the newsagent asked.

"He might be if we don't find him," I replied.

"But he won't necessarily be if we do," Herbert added unnecessarily.

The newsagent hesitated. He didn't trust us. If I had been him, I wouldn't have trusted us either. Just then the door opened and somebody else came in—to buy a pack of cigarettes or something. "Look, I don't have time to waste with you two jokers," the newsagent said. "You want to speak to the dwarf, you'll find him at the Hotel Splendide at the bottom of the Portobello Road."

"How do you know?" I said.

"I know the owner. He told me he had a dwarf staying there."

"And what's the owner's name?" Herbert asked.

"Jack Splendide."

The farther you go down the Portobello Road, the crummier it gets. It's just about okay until you reach the Electric Cinema, but after that it's downhill all the way. You come to an overpass at the bottom, by which time you're in a different world. You've left the antique shops and the bustling stalls behind you. Now you're in a flat wasteland, up to your ankles in litter. It's amazing how quickly a short walk can take you from one side of London to the other.

The Hotel Splendide was the sort of place that would be hard to find unless you knew it was there—perhaps the sort of place you might choose if you didn't want to be found. It was right at the far end of the Portobello Road, halfway down a narrow cul-de-sac, nestling in the armpit of the overpass, which swept around the building as if holding it in a clammy, concrete embrace. You wouldn't get much sleep at the Hotel Splendide, not with the traffic roaring past only a couple of yards from your bedroom window. Because the top floor of the building, beneath the flat roof, was level with the raised highway. Roll over in bed and you risked being run over by a truck. That is, if the bedbugs and cockroaches didn't get to you first.

It was a square, ugly building, the color of moldy cheese. A red neon sign with the name glowed behind a first-floor window, only the glass was so dirty you could hardly read it. A row of garbage cans stood outside the entrance, their overflowing garbage adding to the delightful atmosphere. You know how some travel guides award symbols of knives and forks to hotels in recognition of their quality? Well, the Hotel Splendide wouldn't even have merited a toothpick.

There was a drunk lying half asleep next to the garbage cans, the top of a wine bottle poking out of the brown paper bag that he clutched in one hand. A dog—an Alsatian—lay sprawled beside him. It was drunk, too. We stepped past them and went into the hotel. The door was hanging off its hinges. The interior smelled of sweat and disinfectant.

We found ourselves in what passed for a reception area. Some hotels advertise theaters and restaurants. In this one the posters advertised soup kitchens and delousing clinics. There was a counter opposite the door, and behind it an unshaven man reading a cheap paperback. He was wearing a grimy shirt and jeans with a stomach that managed to force its way over the top of the belt and sag down to his thighs. He was sucking on a cigar that had gone out perhaps a week ago. He didn't look up as we approached. Instead, he flicked a page in his book, grunted, and went on reading.

"You Jack Splendide?" Herbert asked.

"Who wants to know?" He talked without moving his lips. But the cigar waggled between his teeth.

"The name's Diamond," Herbert said. "I'm a private eye."

"Ya don't say!" Splendide yawned and went back to the book.

"We're looking for someone who's staying here," I explained. "A dwarf. His name's Johnny Naples. He owes a client of ours a lot of bread."

"That's right," Herbert said. "And if we find him, we'll cut you in for a slice."

We were making it all up, of course, but it was the only way to get past the hotel manager. He jerked a thumb in the direction of the stairs. "Room thirty-nine," he said.

We climbed five flights of stairs, trying to stop them from creaking beneath our feet. The carpet was threadbare, the walls damp and discolored. We could hear TV sets blaring away in the distance and a baby crying. I suppose I'd have cried, too, if I'd had to stay there. Room 39 was at the back of the hotel, at the bottom of a corridor. We guessed it was 39 because it came after 37 and 38. But the number had fallen off. The door was closed.

"Do you think this is a good idea?" Herbert whispered.

"Have you got a better one?" I asked.

"We could go home . . ."

"Come on, Tim," I said. "We've found him now. It can't hurt to—"

That was as far as I got. The gunshot wasn't loud, but it was close enough to make me jump the way you do when a car backfires or somebody drops a plate. It had come from the other side of the door. Herbert froze, then tried to lurch away, but fortunately I managed to grab hold of his jacket. I didn't want to go into the room by myself. I didn't want to go into the room at all. But if I'd run away then, I'd never have forgiven myself.

Still clutching Herbert, I opened the door. It wasn't locked. In the Hotel Splendide, the rooms didn't have locks. Some of them didn't even have doors.

The first thing I saw was a flapping curtain and a shadowy figure disappearing outside. I couldn't even tell if it was a man or a woman. There was just the flash of a leg hanging over the edge of the sill and then it was gone.

It was a small room, just big enough for a bed, a table, a chest of drawers, and a corpse. I closed the door behind me. Johnny Naples was lying on the bed. He wasn't dead yet, but the big red splotch on his shirt told me that his time was running out about as quickly as his blood. I went over to the window and looked outside. But I was too late. Whoever had climbed out had jumped the short distance to the overpass and run for it. Maybe they'd had a car waiting for them. Anyway, they were gone.

The dwarf groaned and I looked back again. The room was probably in a mess to begin with, but I guessed there had been a fight. There was a chair upturned on the floor and a lamp had been knocked over on the table. My eyes fell on a pack of matches. I don't know why I picked them up and put them in my pocket. I knew we didn't have a lot of time and that any clue—no matter how small—might help. Maybe it was just that I didn't want to look at the dwarf. Anyway, that's what I did.

Johnny Naples opened his mouth and tried to speak.

"The falcon . . ." he said. Then a nasty, bubbling sound.

Then: "The sun . . ." And that was it. His eyes closed. The mouth stayed open.

D for "dwarf." *D* for "dead."

Herbert had picked something up off the carpet.

"Nick . . ." he began.

It was a gun. And it was still smoking.

And he was still standing there, holding it, when the door crashed open. The man who had been drunk outside the Hotel Splendide was standing there and he had a gun, too. The Alsatian was with him, growling softly.

There were two more people behind him.

"Police!" he shouted.

Herbert fainted.

The man swung around to cover him. "You're under arrest," he said.

THE FALCON

Johnny Naples was taken to the morgue. We were taken to the Ladbroke Grove Police Station. I don't know which of us got the better treatment. While he was carried out on his back, covered with a nice clean sheet, we were dragged out, handcuffed together, and thrown into the back of a van. It had turned out, of course, that the drunk in the street had been a plainclothes policeman. The Alsatian was a plainclothes police dog. The Hotel Splendide had been the subject of a major police stakeout, and we'd more or less asked for trouble the moment we'd walked in.

We were left to stew in a bare-bricked interrogation room. Or to freeze, rather. That place couldn't have been much warmer than the morgue. There was one metal table, three metal chairs, and five metal bars on a window that would have been too small to climb out of anyway. A blackboard lined one wall and there was a poster on the other reading CRIME DOESN'T PAY, underneath which somebody had scrawled NEITHER DOES POLICE WORK. The room smelled of stale cigarette smoke. I wondered how many hardened criminals had grown harder waiting there.

Herbert had said little since he woke up. But after about

twenty minutes he suddenly looked around as if he had only just realized where he was. "Nick . . . ?" he said.

"Yes?"

"You don't think the police think I had anything to do with what happened to the dwarf, do you?" he asked.

"No," I replied soothingly. "You went up to see him. There was a gunshot. You were found holding a smoking gun. The dwarf was dead. Why would the police think you're involved?"

At that moment there was a rattle as a key was turned in the lock and the door swung open. Herbert groaned. The man who had just come in didn't look too happy either.

"Herbert Simple," he said.

"Inspector Snape," Herbert muttered in a strangled voice.

"Chief Inspector Snape," the man growled. "No thanks to you."

The chief inspector was blond-haired and built like a football player, with those slightly squashed shoulders that come from too many tackles. His skin was the color of raw bacon and he spoke with a northern accent. He was wearing an off-white shirt that had probably been pure white when he put it on, and a tie that had slipped over his collar in its struggle to get away from his bulging neck. He was followed by a smaller, squatter version of himself with black, permed hair, an open-neck shirt, and a gold medallion glittering in the forest of his chest. The assistant—if that's what he was—stood there, pounding one fist into the palm of his hand, looking at us with unfriendly, muddy brown eyes. Well, if these are the cops, I thought, I'd hate to meet the robbers.

"Herbert Simple," Snape repeated, drawing up a chair.

"Can I hit him?" the other policeman asked.

"No, Boyle." The chief inspector smiled unpleasantly. "Herbert Simple." He said the name a third time, chewing on the words like they were stuck in his teeth. "The worst police constable that ever served in my station. In two months you did more damage than the Kray brothers managed in twenty years. The day you left, I cried like a baby. Tears of pleasure. I never thought . . . I hoped, I prayed that I would never see you again." His piglike eyes were turned on me. "And who are you, laddie?" he asked.

"His brother," I said.

"Bad luck, son. Bad luck."

"Can I hit *him*?" Boyle asked.

"Relax, Boyle." The chief inspector took out a cigarette and lit it. "Now, the question I'm asking myself is, why should a luckless, hopeless, brainless ex-policeman like Herbert Simple be mixed up with a man like Johnny Naples?"

"I didn't shoot him!" Herbert cried.

"I believe you." Snape's nostrils quivered as they blew out two streams of smoke. "If you'd wanted to shoot the dwarf, you'd have probably missed and shot yourself in the foot. After all, when we sent you for target practice, you managed to shoot the instructor. But the fact still remains that your fingerprints are on the gun—and nobody else's. So perhaps you'd better tell me what you were doing there."

"Naples was my client," Herbert squeaked.

"Your client?"

"He's a private detective," I explained.

"A private detective?" Chief Inspector Snape began to laugh. He laughed until the tears trickled down his checks. At last he managed to calm himself down, wiping his eyes with the back of his hand. Boyle handed him a handkerchief and he blew his nose noisily. "Now I've heard everything!" he said. "A private detective. And your client's dead. That makes sense. The moment he came to you he was a marked man. But what private detection did Naples want?"

"It's private," I said.

That wiped the smile off Snape's face. At the same time, Boyle grunted and lumbered toward me. I'd seen prettier sights in the London Zoo. Fortunately for me, Snape held up a hand. "Forget it, Boyle," he snapped.

"But, Chief . . ."

"He's underage."

Boyle grunted again and punched the air. But he hung back.

"You should watch yourself, son," Snape said. "Boyle here is very into police brutality. He watches too much TV. The last suspect we had in here ended up in intensive care and he was just in for double parking."

"It's still private," I said.

"All right," Snape grumbled. "If you want to see your big brother arrested for murder . . ."

"Nick . . . !" Herbert whimpered.

"Wait a minute," I said. "We don't have to break a client's confidence."

"Your client's dead," Snape said.

"I noticed. But he's still our client." I gave him my friend-liest smile. "Look, Chief Inspector," I said. "You tell us what you know and we'll tell you what we know. That seems fair to me."

Snape looked at me thoughtfully. "How old are you?" he asked.

"Thirteen."

"You're smart for your age. If you go on as smart as this, maybe you won't reach fourteen."

"Just tell us."

"Why should I? How do I know you know anything at all."

"We know about the key," I said. "And about the falcon."

I admit they were two shots in the dark. The Fat Man had mentioned a key, and with his dying breath Johnny Naples had muttered something about a falcon. Neither of them made any sense to me, but I had gambled that they would mean something to this Snape character. And I was right. He had raised an eyebrow at the mention of the key. The other one joined it when I followed with the falcon.

He finished the cigarette, dropped the butt, and ground it

out with his heel. "Okay," he said. "But you'd better be on the level, Nick. Otherwise I'll let Boyle spend a little time alone with you."

Boyle looked at me like he was trying to work out a new pattern for my face.

"Johnny Naples flew in here from South America a month ago," Snape began. "We picked him up when he came through passport control, then we lost him, then—just a few days ago—we found him again at the Hotel Splendide. We've had him under observation ever since. You and your brother were the first people to see him, as far as we know. He never went out—not while we were watching."

"Why were you watching him?" Herbert asked.

"That's what I'm trying to tell you," Snape snapped. He lit himself another cigarette. He didn't look like a chain-smoker, but that's the sort of effect my big brother has on people. "Johnny Naples was a nobody," Snape went on. "A quack doctor with a run-down practice in the backstreets of La Paz, Bolivia. But with his last patient he got lucky. You already know about the Falcon, but I wonder how much you know? His full name, for example—Henry von Falkenberg. I reckon he was out of your league. To be fair, von Falkenberg was in a league of his own.

"Look—every country has its big crooks. In England, the Fat Man is probably number one. America has its godfathers. In Italy, there are the Fettuccine brothers. But the Falcon—he's an internationalist. He was half English and half German, loyal to neither country, and living, when we last heard of him, in Bolivia. There wasn't a single criminal organization in the world that he wasn't doing business with. You steal a truckload of mink coats in Moscow? You sell it to the Falcon. You want to buy a kilo of cocaine in Canada? Just have a word with the Falcon. He was the number one, the top man, the king of crime. If there was a country in the world where the police didn't want him, he'd have taken it as a personal insult.

"Now, like any big businessman, the Falcon needed funds—a financial platform on which to build his deals. But unlike most businessmen, he couldn't just open an account at your local credit union. He didn't trust the Swiss banks. He didn't trust his own mother—which is probably why he had her rubbed out back in 1965. The only currency the Falcon would deal in was diamonds: uncut diamonds. The franc might fall, the ruble might rise—but diamonds held their own. In every major city he had his own little stash of diamonds: in Paris, Amsterdam, New York . . . and London. In fact, London was the center of his operations, so that's where he had the biggest stash. We can't be sure, but we believe that perhaps only a mile from here, he'd managed to conceal diamonds to the value of five million dollars."

He paused for effect and he got it. I licked my lips. Herbert shook his head and whistled.

"The Falcon was a great criminal," Snape continued. "But a month ago his luck ran out. He could have been arrested. He could have been machine-gunned by a rival gang. But in the end he was run over by a bus. It was a crazy end to a crazy life. It happened just outside La Paz airport as he crossed the road to catch a plane to England. We believe he was carrying the key to the diamonds with him. And the man who just happened to be on the scene, who traveled with him in the ambulance on the way to the hospital, was Johnny Naples.

"So the Falcon is lying on his back with the life running out of him and he—and only he—knows where a fortune in diamonds is hidden. Now, we can't be certain, but people who are dying tend to blurt out secrets that they would otherwise keep to themselves, and we believe the Falcon told Johnny Naples where he could find those diamonds. Look at it this way. A few days later, Naples dumps his job and takes a first-class flight to London. There's no reason why he should have come here unless you put two and two together and make—"

"Five million," I said.

"Right." Snape stood up and walked over to the blackboard. He had produced a piece of chalk from his pocket. "So Johnny Naples flies to the end of the rainbow—in this case, England. But he's not alone. Because all sorts of people are interested in the diamonds now that the Falcon is dead." He turned around and scrawled a name on the blackboard.

The Fat Man

"He's number one. The Fat Man had often done business with the Falcon. If anybody knew about the secret stash, it would be him. And he could use the money. Give the Fat Man five million dollars and maybe he could go international himself. He could become the next Falcon. He probably knew where the dwarf was staying before we did. Did he kill Johnny Naples? If so, he'll be on his way to the diamonds . . . and that's bad news for all of us."

Snape wrote a second name beneath it.

Beatrice von Falkenberg

"She's the dark horse," Snape continued. "The Falcon's wife—his widow—once Holland's greatest actress. He fell in love with her when he saw her in *Othello*. She played the title role. From all accounts it wasn't a happy marriage. She spent six months of the year in London and six months in La Paz. Did he ever tell her where the diamonds were hidden? If he didn't, she'll want to know . . ."

Two more names followed.

William Gott and Eric Himmell

"They were the Falcon's right-hand men, his two lieutenants. If they could get their hands on the diamonds, they'd have enough money and enough power to take over the Falcon's empire. Gott and Himmell are killers. Although they were born in Germany, they were both educated in England, at Eton. During that time, the vicar and the PE instructor went missing and the assistant headmaster was found hanged with his own old school tie. They arrived in London the day after Johnny Naples. They're here now, and they're deadly."

The Professor

"He's another mystery. But if anybody knows where the diamonds are, it's likely to be him. He was the Falcon's technical adviser, his tame egghead. He was brilliant but crooked. For example, he invented computer fraud five years before someone invented the computer. If the diamonds are in some sort of safe, he'll probably have built it. But about a year ago he went missing. He could be dead. Nobody's heard of him since then."

Snape turned to the blackboard and wrote a final name.

Herbert Simp

That was as far as he got. The chalk broke in his hand.

"And at last we come to you," he said. "Hopeless, horrible Herbert Simple. You say Johnny Naples was your client. I want to know why. I want to know what he wanted. I want to know what he said. I want to know what you two are doing mixed up in all this and I want to know now!"

He paused.

Things were beginning to make some sort of sense. Not a lot of sense, mind you, but at least we knew what stakes we were playing for. Johnny Naples had come to London in search of five million dollars and he had left us a box of Maltesers. It wasn't a lot to go on, but it was all we had. The trouble was, if we told Snape what Naples had given us, we'd lose that, too. The way I saw it was like this. A lot of people were interested in what had taken place in our office that Thursday morning. The Fat Man was one of them. And perhaps it had been Gott and Himmell who had ransacked the place that same night. Sooner or later they'd come gunning for us, and if worse came to worst, we'd have to give them the Maltesers. Which meant we had to keep them from Snape.

And—okay—I'll be honest. If we were really sitting on the key to a fortune, I wanted to be the one to turn it. There were plenty of things I could do with five million dollars. I figured I'd let Herbert keep the other half.

"Come on," Snape growled. "It's your turn. What did Naples want?"

There was another long silence. Boyle shuffled forward and I noticed that this time Snape made no move to stop him.

"Naples came here looking for the money," I said. "You were right there. But he was followed. He was afraid. That's why he came to see us. He thought we'd be able to give him some sort of protection."

"Nick!" Herbert muttered.

"He didn't tell us anything more than that . . ."

Boyle's hand clamped down on the back of my neck. He half dragged me to my feet. Now I knew how a piece of scrap iron feels when it's picked up by a mechanical grabber. I waited for him to crush me. "You're lying," he rasped.

"Scout's honor!" I pleaded.

"You knew about the key," Snape reminded me.

"Only because Naples mentioned it. But we haven't got it. You can search the office if you like."

"We already have," Boyle said.

"Then you'll know that somebody tore it apart. Look—if we knew anything, why do you think we went to the Hotel Splendide? The place was searched and we got scared. We went to see Naples to ask him what was going on, but by the time we got there, he was dead. Honest!"

For a moment the only sound in the room was a vague creaking as my neck splintered in Boyle's grip. But then he must have gotten some sort of signal from Snape. He released me and I collapsed in my chair. My legs had turned to jelly. I could hardly move my head.

"Okay, we'll play it your way, son," Snape said humorlessly. "We'll let you go. But I don't believe you and neither will the Fat Man or any of the other nasties waiting for you out there. It'll be interesting to see which one of them gets to you first."

"And I suppose you'll stand by and watch," I muttered, rubbing my neck.

"Don't worry," Snape said. "We'll be around to pick up the pieces."

GRANNIES

It's funny how the smell of police stations sticks on you long after you've gone. Snape was decent enough to get a police car to take us home and we carried the smell with us, down past the Albert Hall and through Earl's Court. They say that good detectives have a "nose" for crime. They "sniff" out clues, and when things are going well, they're on the right "scent." After a couple of hours in the Ladbroke Grove interrogation room, I could see what they mean. The strong arm of the law could do with a strong underarm deodorant.

We had a bath when we got in and changed into fresh clothes. Then Herbert suggested we should go out and get something to eat. I didn't argue. He'd been very quiet since we'd walked in on the dead dwarf and I could tell something was brewing. Perhaps he was finally going to pack in the private-detective business and send me packing, too. All the same, I dug up the Maltesers from beneath the floorboard and took them with me. That was funny, too. Before, when I hadn't known what they were worth, I'd slung them about like you would any box of candy. Now that I knew they carried a five-million-dollar price tag, I could feel them burning a hole in my pocket.

We walked down the Fulham Road toward Kensington

Station. Herbert was still quiet. And he was jumpy. When a guy stopped us to ask us the time, Herbert jumped, disappearing behind a parked car. I found him there a minute later, crouching down, pretending to tie his shoelaces. It would have been a bit more convincing if his shoes had had laces. The truth was, Herbert was afraid, certain we were being watched. The taxi driver on the other side of the road, the old man walking his dog, the couple kissing at the bus stop . . . as far as Herbert was concerned, any one of them could have been working for the Fat Man, for Beatrice von Falkenberg, for the police . . . whoever.

We stopped at a fast-food restaurant called Grannies. It got the name because all the hamburgers were served in granary-bread buns. As a sort of publicity stunt, someone had also had the bright idea of only employing grannies—little old ladies with gray hair and glasses. The only trouble with all this was that for a fast-food restaurant, it was actually pretty slow. The chef must have been about a hundred and two. One of the waitresses used a walker. But the food's okay and we were in no hurry. We took a table by the window. Herbert chose the chair that looked out. There was no way he was going to sit with his back to the street.

We ordered Grannyburgers and fries with chocolate milk shakes on the side and hardly said anything until it all arrived. I picked up the ketchup holder and squeezed it. The stuff spat out, missing the plate and splattering onto the white table. It looked like blood.

Herbert put down his knife and fork. "Nick . . ." he began.

Herbert?" I said expectantly. Actually, I knew what to expect now. I should have seen it coming.

"This case is getting out of hand," he said. "I mean . . . it's getting dangerous. The way things are going, I reckon somebody could soon get hurt."

"You mean—like Johnny Naples?" I reminded him.

"Right." Herbert stared at the ketchup, his lip curling. "And he wasn't just hurt," he went on. "I mean, he probably was hurt. But he was also killed."

"You can't get more hurt than that," I agreed.

He nodded. "So what I'm saying is, maybe it's time you split. You're a good kid, Nick. But you're only thirteen. This is a case for Tim Diamond."

It was incredible. Maybe it was the shock of what had happened that day or maybe it was the milk shake, but Herbert was trying to get rid of me. "This is a case for Tim Diamond"—it was a line out of a bad movie, but Herbert really believed it. I could see him switching into his private-detective role even as he sat there, shoulders slumped, eyes hard. He'd have had a cigarette dangling out of the corner of his mouth if cigarettes didn't make him throw up.

"I figure I'll send you to Auntie Maureen in Slough," he went on. I shuddered. Auntie Maureen, my mother's sister, had a semidetached house and a semidetached artificial hip. She was only fifty years old but was in need of round-the-clock nursing. Whenever I stayed with her, I ended up as her round-the-clock nurse. "Or you could always go to Australia and stay with Mum and Dad," Herbert added.

I took a deep breath and pronged a forkful of french fries. Whenever Herbert got into these moods, I had to tread carefully. If I ever suggested that the great Tim Diamond needed any help from his thirteen-year-old brother, I'd have been on the next plane to Sydney faster than you could whistle "Waltzing Malteser."

"It's nice of you to think of me, Tim," I said. "And I don't want to get in your way. But I reckon I'd be safer with you."

"Safer?" He took a bite out of his burger.

"Sure. I mean, the Fat Man could come for me in Slough. I might get kidnapped, or brutally beaten with Auntie Maureen's artificial hip."

"That's true."

"But I feel safe with you," I continued. "Back in the Hotel Splendide, for example. I don't know what I'd have done without you."

Herbert smiled modestly.

"The way you fainted. It was . . . heroic."

Now he scowled. "You're not goofing on me, are you?"

"Me? No way."

I felt it was time to bring the conversation to a close, so I took out the box of Maltesers and put them on the table.

"That's what we should be worrying about," I said. "Five million dollars, Herbert. And it's our only clue."

"I don't get it," Herbert said. Herbert never did.

"Look . . ." I spoke slowly, trying to make it easy for him. "Johnny Naples comes to England with the key to a fortune. That's what the Fat Man asked us for—remember? A key. Now, all Johnny's got is this box of Maltesers, but maybe he doesn't know what it means either."

"How do you know that?" Herbert asked.

"Because Snape told us that the dwarf had been in England for a whole month before he was killed. Maybe the Falcon didn't have time to tell him everything before he died. Naples had a rough idea and came over here to look."

"Go on."

"All right. So Naples comes to England. He checks into the Hotel Splendide. And he starts looking. But unfortunately for him, there are lots of people interested in him. The same people who are now interested in us. But Johnny Naples still manages to find out what the Maltesers mean. He takes them with him—like you'd take a treasure map. So that nobody will see what he's carrying, he buys an envelope to put them in. He goes from the hotel to Fulham. But then he sees that he's being followed. So what does he do?"

"I don't know," Herbert said breathlessly. "What does he do?"

"He comes to us. He's in the street and he happens to see your name on the door. You're a private detective. That's perfect. And maybe your name rings a bell."

"No, Nick," Herbert interrupted. "It's the little button by the door that rings the bell . . ."

"No," I groaned. "I mean Tim *Diamond*. Diamonds are what this is all about."

"Oh—I see."

"Johnny Naples comes in and gives us the envelope. You remember how scared he was? He knew that he was being followed. So he gives us the package—which is what everybody wants—and promises to come back when the heat is off."

"But he didn't come back," Herbert said.

"No. Because he got killed."

"Not to mention hurt!"

"And now we've got the Maltesers. And if we can work out where he was going and what he was going to do with them when he got there, we'll be rich."

"That's terrific!" Herbert exclaimed. As I had hoped, all thoughts of Slough and Auntie Maureen had left his head. Quickly, he finished his meal. Then he picked up the box. "Perhaps the diamonds are inside," he suggested. "Covered in chocolate."

"No," I said. "I doubt if you could fit five million dollars' worth inside, and anyway, I've already eaten six of them and they certainly didn't taste like diamonds."

"What do diamonds taste like?"

"That's not the point, Herbert!"

"So what is the point?"

It was a good question. You can go and buy a box of Maltesers in any candy store, but to save you the money, let me just describe the box we had. It had the name of the candy written in white letters on a red background, surrounded by pictures of the chocolate balls themselves. This was on the top and on all four sides. On one side it also carried the inspiring message *the lighter way to enjoy chocolates* and on the other, the weight: *146g 5.15 oz.*

There was more on the bottom. It read *chocolates with crisp, light honeycombed centers* and then there was the usual blurb about the milk solids and the vegetable fat that had achieved this miracle. In addition there was a guarantee: *This product should reach you in perfect condition* . . . and a line asking you to keep your country tidy.

After that, there was a red code number—*MLB 493*— and, in a red panel, *best before 28-12-08.* In the left-hand corner, painted in blue, was the bar code, the series of thick and thin lines that you get on all products these days. There was a number beneath that, too: *3521 201 000000.* And that is about as complete a description of a box of Maltesers as you are ever going to find in a library or bookshop.

It was not very helpful.

The waitress hobbled over and we ordered two Granny-pies. We sat in silence, waiting for them to arrive. The question was, how could you hide the location of a fortune in diamonds on a box of candy—and for that matter, why choose a box of candy in the first place? The answer was in our hands and even then I might have been able to guess, for the truth is, I had forgotten one important detail. One thing that Johnny Naples had done had slipped my mind. I was still trying to work it out when Herbert spoke.

"Any luck?" he asked.

"No."

We finished our dessert and asked for the bill.

"How about the little dots?" Herbert asked.

"Little dots?"

"Under the letters." He pointed at the Maltesers. "They could spell out another message."

"But there aren't any little dots," I said.

"They could be written in invisible ink."

"I can't see it."

"That's because it's invisible." He smiled triumphantly.

"Listen," I said. "If Johnny Naples didn't know what the Maltesers meant, he'd have had to find out—right?"

"Right," Herbert agreed.

"So if we can work out where he went while he was in England, maybe we'll find out, too."

"Right." Herbert frowned. "But he's dead. So where do we start?"

"Maybe here," I said.

I took out the book of matches that I had found in the

hotel and gave it to him. They belonged to a place called the Casablanca Club with an address in the West End. There was a map on the inside of the cover and three matches left.

"Where did you get this?" Herbert asked.

"I picked it up in the dwarf's room at the hotel," I said. "I thought it might be useful."

"Yes." Herbert considered. "We'll go there tomorrow," he said. "If we can work out where Johnny Naples went while he was in England, maybe we can find out what the Maltesers mean."

I nearly choked on my milk shake. "That's brilliant!" I exclaimed.

"Sure thing, kid," Herbert said.

I didn't remind him that I'd said exactly the same thing only a few moments before. But neither did he remind me about Slough or Mum and Dad. This might be a case for Tim Diamond, but as long as I played my cards right, it seemed there was still room for his little brother, Nick.

THE CASABLANCA CLUB

We were woken up at nine the next morning by the engineer who'd come to fix the phone and we just had time to fall asleep again before we were woken up by Betty Charlady, who'd come to fix the apartment. She had brought with her a bag of tools and was soon assembling Herbert's desk, hammering away at the wood with a mouth full of nails. It seemed incredible that she should do all this for a lousy ten dollars a day, but I assumed I brought out the motherly instinct in her. Strange how I could never do the same for my mother.

While Herbert got dressed and shaved, I nipped out for eggs, milk, and bread. We hadn't had time to cash the check and money was running low, so I had to squeeze more credit out of the supermarket owner. The owner, Mr. Patel, is a decent old stick. He also owns a decent old stick, which he tried to hit me with as I ran out without paying, but at least I was able to rustle up a decent breakfast for Herbert and me, and a cup of tea for Mrs. Charlady.

After breakfast, Herbert rang the Casablanca Club and I discovered that it would be open that night—although to members only. Betty Charlady was screwing a chair back together in the office at the time and she must have overheard the call, because when she came into the kitchen she was scowling.

"Wassis Casablanca Club?" she asked.

"It's in Charing Cross," I said. "We're going there tonight."

"You shouldn't do it, Master Nicholas," Betty muttered. "At your age."

I handed her a cup of tea. She took it and sat down, her eyes searching across the table for a biscuit. "It's part of our investigation," I explained. "A client of ours may have gone there, so we have to go there, too."

But Mrs. Charlady wasn't impressed. "These London clubs," she said. "They're just dens of innik-witty." She shook her head and the gray curls of her hair tumbled like lemmings off a cliff. "You go if you have to. But I'm sure no good will come of it . . ."

Nonetheless, Herbert and I made our way to the Casablanca Club that same night, arriving just after twelve. There's a corner of Charing Cross, just behind the station, that comes straight out of the nineteenth century. As the road slopes down toward the river, you leave the traffic and the bright lights behind you and suddenly the night seems to creep up on you and grab you by the collar. Listen carefully and you'll hear the Thames water gurgling in the distance, and as you squint into the shadows you'll see figures shuffling slowly past like zombies. For this is down-and-out territory.

Old tramps and winos wander down and pass out underneath the arches at the bottom, wrapped in filthy raincoats and the day's headlines.

The Casablanca Club was in the middle of all this. A flight of steps led down underneath a dimmed green bulb, and if you didn't know what you were looking for, there was no way you'd find it. There was no name, no fancy sign. Only the tinkle of piano music that seemed to seep out of the cracks in the pavement hinted that in the dirt and the dust and the darkness of Charing Cross, somebody might be having a good time.

We climbed down to a plain wooden door about fifteen feet below the level of the pavement. Somebody must have been watching through the spyhole because it opened before we had time to knock.

"Yes?" a voice said.

Friendly place, I thought.

"Can we come in?" Herbert asked.

"You members?"

"No."

"Then beat it!"

The door swung shut. At the last moment, Herbert managed to get his foot in the crack. There was a nasty crunching sound as his shoe, and possibly his foot, too, got chewed up in the woodwork, but then the door swung open again and I managed to push my way through and into the hall. A bald man in a dinner jacket gave me an ugly look. If he ever wanted to give anyone a pretty look, he'd need major plastic surgery.

"We're friends of Johnny Naples," I said.

The man shrugged. "Why didn't you say so before?" he asked.

"You didn't ask," I said.

He opened the door again. Herbert was writhing on the concrete outside, clutching his mangled foot. "Instant membership—ten bucks," the bald man said. He glanced at me. "You're underage," he muttered.

"You don't look too good yourself," I replied.

"How old are you?" he asked.

"Twenty-five."

"Twenty-five?" He sneered. "You got a driver's license?"

"No. I got a chauffeur."

I walked on, leaving Herbert to find the money and pay. In the dim light I could have been any age. Anyway, I was taller than Johnny Naples had ever been and they'd allowed him in.

Funnily enough, the first waiter who saw me mistook me for the dwarf in the half-light. "Mr. Naples!" The words were two drops of oil squeezed into my ear and I was led to a table at the front of a large room. There was such a thick haze in the air that my eyes had more water in them than the house whiskey. I loosened my tie and sat down. It felt like there was more smoke in the air than there was air in the smoke. Another waiter passed. "Good evening, Mr. Naples."

He put a silver bucket and two glasses on the table. I leaned forward. There was a bottle of champagne in the bucket, surrounded by ice cubes, already uncorked. "With the compliments of the house," the waiter said. I scratched my head. The dwarf must have been quite a regular here. Came regular, drank regular . . . I wondered what else he did regular at the Casablanca Club.

I looked around me. There were perhaps a hundred people there, sitting at tables or crowding around the bar, where three black-tied waiters shook cocktails behind a curving marble counter. The air was filled with the hubbub of conversation, as thick and as indistinct as the cigarette smoke. There was a dance floor at one end, but tonight there was no band, just a black pianist stroking the ivories with fingers that looked too stubby to sound so good. Right in front of my table there was a stage about the size you'd expect a stage to be in a run-down drinking club. The place had no windows and no ventilation. The smoke had smothered the light, strangled the plants, and it wasn't doing a lot for me either.

I ignored the champagne and poured myself a glass of water out of the ice bucket. Herbert joined me, muttering about the ten bucks and a moment later a spotlight cut through the clouds and the crowd fell silent. A figure moved onto the stage, a woman in her fifties, who dressed like she was in her thirties, with jewelry flashing here and there to keep your eyes off the wrinkles. She was attractive if you didn't look too closely. At one time she might even have been beautiful. But the years hadn't been good to her. They'd taken the color out of her hair, put a husk in her voice, hollowed out her throat, and slapped her around a bit for good measure.

Fumes from all the cigarettes were still swirling around me and I was beginning to understand what passive smoking was all about. Spend too long in here and I'd start wheezing and my fingers would turn yellow.

The pianist had come to the end of a tune, but as the woman moved forward he began another and she sang almost as if she didn't care what she was doing. She sang two or three songs. When she finished, she got a smattering of applause, and as the talk started up again, she moved down to our table and sat opposite me. Only when she was close enough to see the pinks of my eyes (the whites had gone that color in all the smoke) did she see who I was.

"You're not Johnny," she said.

"We're friends of his . . ." I said. I let the sentence hang in the air. I needed her name to complete it.

"Lauren Bacardi," she said. "Where's Johnny?"

I looked at Herbert. From the way she was talking, the little guy had obviously meant something to her and I didn't know how she would take the news. I hoped he'd think of a gentle way to tell her. You know, with a bit of tact.

"He's dead," Herbert said.

"Dead?"

"Yup." He nodded. "Dead."

She took out a cigarette and lit it. I guessed she needed something to do with her hands. After all, to smoke in the unique atmosphere of the Casablanca Club, you didn't actually need to light another cigarette. "Was he . . . killed?" she asked.

"Yeah," I said. I drank some iced water. It tasted like the metal bucket it had come from. "You knew him?"

She smiled sadly. "We were friends." Her eyes clouded over. Or maybe it was just the cigarette smoke. I thought she was going to get up and walk out of our lives. The way things turned out, it would have been better if she had. But the pianist had slid into a bluesy number and she needed to talk. "Johnny and I knew each other for ten years," she said. "But we never met. Not until a month ago.

"We were pen pals. He was in South America. I was over here. Maybe you'll laugh at me, but we kind of fell in love by mail." She flicked ash onto the carpet. "We wrote letters to each other for ten years and he never even mentioned that he was a dwarf. I only found out a month ago, when he came over, and by then I'd more or less agreed to marry him. The little rat . . ."

She puffed at her cigarette. The smoke in the room grew a little thicker. Herbert waved a hand in front of his face. I knew how he felt.

"He came over," she went on. "He just turned up one day on my doormat. No. He was standing on a chair on the doormat—to reach the bell. He had these plans. We were going to be rich. We'd buy this little house in the South of France with low ceilings. Johnny didn't like high ceilings. He told me that he knew where he could lay his hands on five million dollars—enough money to take me away from all this . . ."

She raised her hands, taking in the whole of the Casablanca Club with ten chipped and nicotine-stained fingernails.

"Did he have anything with him?" I asked. "A box, for example?"

"You mean the Maltesers?" Lauren Bacardi smiled. "Sure. He never went anywhere without them. He seemed to think they were important, but he didn't know why. It nearly drove him mad . . . if he wasn't mad already. I mean, how could a box of candy be worth all that dough?"

She paused. "But maybe he was on the level," Lauren went on. "Why else would anyone want to wipe him out? I mean, Johnny never hurt anyone in his life. He was too small.

"And he was afraid—all the time he was in England. He wouldn't stay at my place. He hid himself away in some filthy pit of a hotel, and whenever we went out together, he always made like he was being followed. I thought he was imagining things." A single tear trickled down her cheek, turning a muddy brown as it picked up her makeup. "Just my luck," she whispered. "Johnny getting himself killed just one day after he'd found the answer."

"He found the diamonds?" Herbert cried.

"No." She shook her head. "Just the answer. We were out together one day and he saw something; something that made everything make sense."

"What was it?" Herbert and I asked more or less together.

"Miss Bacardi?" the waiter interrupted. "There's someone at the door with some flowers for you."

"For me?" She got to her feet, swaying slightly in front of us. "Just give me one minute."

She moved away in the direction of the front entrance, followed by the waiter. Herbert looked at the half-empty bottle of champagne. "Did I pay for that?" he asked.

"It was on the house," I told him.

"What was it doing up there?" he asked.

Neither Herbert nor I said anything for a while, and in that silence I became aware of a little voice whispering in my ear. It wasn't Herbert. It was actually making sense. It was my common sense trying to tell me something was wrong. I played back what had just happened and suddenly I knew what it was. The flowers. Why had the waiter made Lauren Bacardi walk all the way to the entrance instead of bringing them to her? And there was something else. Maybe it was just a coincidence. Maybe it didn't mean anything. But now I remembered. The waiter had spoken with a German accent. I was on my feet making for the door before I knew what I was doing. Herbert ran after me, calling my name. But I wasn't going to stop and explain what was going on. I pushed my way through the crowd, ignoring the shouts of protest and the crash of breaking glass. That was one time I was glad I wasn't fully grown. Before anyone could see me to grab hold of me, I was gone.

I reached the door and the cold night hit me like an angry woman, slapping my face and tearing at my hair. The first thing I saw were the remains of what had been a bouquet of flowers. But now the cellophane was torn and the flowers were scattered over the steps, the stalks broken. At the same time, I heard someone calling out. It was Lauren Bacardi. I took the steps three at a time, and as I reached the street, I just had time to catch sight of her being bundled into the back of a dark blue van. A shadowy figure slammed the door and ran around to the front. The engine was already running. A moment later, so was I.

I ran across to the van, intending . . . I don't know. I guess I thought I'd be able to pull the door open and get Lauren out, but of course it was locked. So instead I jumped onto it, slamming into the metal like a hamburger hitting a griddle, and hung on for dear life as the van roared away. I'd managed to get a foothold of sorts on the license plate and I had one hand on the door handle, one hand curled round the rim at the edge. I was half spread-eagled and traveling at about thirty miles an hour when the van turned a corner. Whoever was driving put their foot down then. Perhaps they'd heard they had an unwelcome passenger. I guess the van was doing sixty when I was thrown off. It was hard to tell. After all, I was sort of somersaulting through the air, and if I'm going to be honest, I might as well add my eyes were tightly closed like I was praying—which, in fact, I was.

All I knew was that me and the van had parted company. It roared off to the left, its tires screaming. I flew off to the right. I could have been killed. I *should* have been killed. But if you go down that part of London at night, you'll find that the offices put a lot of junk out on the pavements, to be cleared up by the garbage trucks the next day. My fall was broken by a mountain of cardboard boxes and plastic bags. Better still, the bags were full of paper that had been put through the shredder; computer printouts and that sort of thing. It was like hitting a pile of cushions. I was bruised. But nothing broke.

A minute later Herbert reached me. He must have been convinced that I was finished because when I got to my feet and walked toward him, brushing strips of paper off my sleeves, he almost fainted with surprise.

"Did you get the van's number?" I asked.

He opened and closed his mouth again without speaking. It was a brilliant impersonation of a goldfish. But I wasn't in the mood to be entertained.

"The license plate . . ." I said.

"No."

"Why not?"

"You were standing on it . . ." He still couldn't believe what he'd just seen.

I looked back down the empty road. Lauren Bacardi had been about to tell us something important and now she was gone. Our only chance of finding the secret of the Maltesers might have gone with her.

"NICE DAY FOR A FUNERAL"

I wasn't feeling too good the next day. I woke up wishing I hadn't, tried to close my eyes, and groaned into the pillow. There was something unpleasant in my mouth. I tried to spit it out, but I couldn't. It was my tongue. Outside, it was raining. I could hear the water pitter-pattering against the windows and dripping through the leak in the bathroom ceiling. I looked out. It was another gray London day with little yellow spots dancing in the air. I figured a couple of Alka-Seltzer would see to the spots, but it looked like we were going to be stuck with the weather.

It took me about twenty minutes to get out of bed. The tumble I had taken the night before must have been harder than I had thought. My right shoulder had gone an interesting shade of black and blue and it hurt when I moved my fingers. Actually it hurt when I moved anything. Somehow I managed to wiggle out of my quilt, and bit by bit, I forced the life back into my battered frame. But it was an hour before I'd made my way downstairs and into the kitchen. It was still raining.

Herbert was sitting there reading a newspaper. When he saw me, he flicked on the kettle and smiled brightly.

"Nice day for a funeral," he said.

"Very funny," I groaned, reaching for the medicine chest.

"I'm being serious." Herbert slid the newspaper in front of me.

I opened the medicine chest—a red plastic box with a white cross on it. It contained two Band-Aids and a tin of cough drops. Clearly Herbert wasn't expecting an outbreak of bubonic plague. I groaned for a second time and pulled the newspaper before me. With an effort, I managed to get the print to unblur itself.

Herbert was right. There was going to be a funeral later in the day—just a few minutes down the road as luck would have it. Or was it luck? I wasn't thinking straight, that was my trouble. The guy being buried was one Henry von Falkenberg. It appeared that the Falcon had flown home.

There was nothing about the Falcon's five million dollars in the paper. They didn't even mention he'd been a crook. In fact it was just one of those fill-in stories, the sort of thing they print between the crossword and the gardening report when they haven't got enough news. This was a story about a wealthy businessman living in Bolivia who had once lived in England and had decided that he wanted to be buried there. The only trouble was, the week he'd died, there'd been a baggage handlers' strike in La Paz and—now that he was dead—"baggage" included him. He'd spent the last four weeks sharing an airport deep freeze with a load of corned beef from Argentina.

But now the strike was over and von Falkenberg could be buried in his family plot just down the road from our apartment. It was too good an opportunity to miss, hungover or not. How many of the names on Snape's blackboard would turn up to pay their last respects to the Falcon?

We had to be there.

Herbert reached for the telephone book. "3521201," he said.

"What's that?" I asked.

"Brompton Cemetery."

I'd written the number down for him and he called them. He spoke briefly before he put down the phone.

"The funeral's at twelve," Herbert said. "Recommended dress: black tie and rain boots."

Perhaps you know Brompton Cemetery—a stretch of ground between Fulham Road and the Brompton Road—a stone's throw away from the soccer field. I sometimes walked there on Sundays, which isn't as creepy as it sounds. After all, there's not much grass in Fulham, and with the sun shining it isn't such a bad place to be. Anyway, the best thing about walking in a cemetery is walking out again. Don't forget, not everyone can.

From the Fulham Road you pass between a pair of tall black iron gates and follow the path. You don't even know you're in a cemetery until you're a short way up and pass the first graves. It's pretty at first. This is the old part of the cemetery, the romantic bit with the grass waist-high and the stones poking out at odd angles like they've grown there, too. Then you turn a corner and there's a cluster of buildings curving around an open space like some sort of weird Victorian summerhouse. Now everything is flat and you can see all the way up to the Brompton Road, a green stretch with the crosses sticking up like the masts of a frozen armada.

We got there at five to twelve, squelching through the rain and the mud, our raincoats pulled up tightly around our necks. About a dozen people had braved the weather to make their farewells to the Falcon . . . and the Argentinian Corned Beef Company had sent a wreath, which was a nice gesture. The first person we met was a less pleasant surprise: Chief Inspector Snape looking about as cheerful as the cemetery's residents. Boyle was behind him, dressed in a crumpled black suit with a mourning band on his arm.

"Simple and Simple," Snape cried, seeing us. "I was planning to visit you as soon as this little shindig was over."

"Why?" Herbert asked.

"We've been receiving reports of an incident in Charing Cross. I thought you might be able to help us with our inquiries into the disappearance of a certain singer. One Lauren Bacardi. It looks like a kidnapping. And guess which kid is our prime suspect?"

"Search me," I said.

"I probably will one of these days," Snape assured me. He smiled at his little joke and I have to admit that jokes don't come much more little than that. "I've got you for murder, for kidnapping, for entering an adult club under false pretenses, and for failing to pay for one bottle of champagne," he went on. "I could lock you up right now."

"You're dead," Boyle whispered.

Snape sighed. "Thank you, Boyle."

"Why don't you arrest us?" I asked.

"Because you're more useful to me outside. I mean, you'd be nice and safe in a cozy police cell, wouldn't you?" He gestured at the other mourners now grouping themselves around the grave. "I'm still waiting to see what happens to you. Come on, Boyle!"

Snape and Boyle went over to the grave. We followed them. It turned out that the Falcon was to be buried in the old part of the cemetery, where the grass was at its highest, the gravestones half buried themselves. There was a vicar standing in the rain beside what looked like some sort of antique telephone booth. It was a stone memorial, about six feet high, mounted by a stone falcon, its beak slightly open, its wings raised. There was a stone tablet set in the memorial below, with a quotation from the Bible cut into it.

THE PATH OF THE JUST IS AS SHINING LIGHT,
THAT SHINETH MORE AND MORE
UNTO THE PERFECT DAY.

Proverbs 4:18

The names of the dead von Falkenbergs were written beneath it: a mother, a father, two grandparents, a cousin . . .

there were seven of them in all. A rectangular hole had been cut into the earth to make room for an eighth. As we approached, the coffin was being lowered. Henry von Falkenberg had come to join his ancestors.

It was raining harder than ever. The vicar had begun the funeral service, but you could hardly hear him for all the splashing. I took the opportunity to examine the other mourners. It was a pity about the weather. What with the umbrellas, the turned-up collars, and the hunched shoulders, it was impossible to see half of them. If the sun had been shining I'd have gotten a better look.

But I did recognize Beatrice von Falkenberg. It had to be her—a tall, elegant woman in black mink with a servant holding an umbrella over her from behind. Her eyes and nose were hidden by a widow's veil, but I could see a pair of thin lips set in an expression of profound boredom. She was dabbing at her eyes with a tiny white handkerchief, but she didn't look too grieved to me. Snape had said that she had been Holland's greatest actress. She wouldn't have won any Oscar for this particular performance.

There was a man standing a short way from her and he caught my attention because he alone carried neither raincoat nor umbrella. He was short and pudgy with silver hair, round glasses in a steel frame, and a face like an owl. As the vicar droned on, he shuffled about on his feet, occasionally steadying himself against a gravestone. Like the widow, he didn't look exactly heartbroken. His eyes were fixed on the von

Falkenberg memorial, but it was easy to see that his mind was miles away.

Who else was there? I recognized a journalist who worked on the local newspaper and who had done a piece on Herbert and me when we'd set up the business. But apart from Snape, Boyle, and the widow, the rest of the crowd were strangers to me. The vicar was hurrying through the service now, tripping over the words to get to the end and out of the rain. His surplice was splashed with mud and pages of his Bible were straggling out of the spine. When he scooped holy dirt into the grave, the wind caught it and threw it back in his eyes. He blinked, spat out an "amen," and ran. Beatrice von Falkenberg turned and went after him. Snape and Boyle hung back. Owl-face jammed his hands into his pockets and sauntered off in the other direction, toward the Brompton Road.

"Very moving. Very touching."

It was a familiar voice and it came from beneath a multi-colored golfing umbrella held by a man who had crept up to stand beside me. I looked round. It was the Fat Man. I should have known that he would be there. "How nice to see you again," he said in a voice that said exactly the opposite.

"Come on," I said to Herbert. I wanted to get back to the apartment, out of the rain.

But the Fat Man blocked my way. "Do you like funerals?" he asked. "I'm thinking of arranging one. Yours."

"I'm too young to die," I said. "What brings you here, Fat Man?"

"Von Falkenberg and I were old friends . . . very dear friends," he explained. "There was something about him that I very much admired—"

"Yeah—his money," I said. "Well, we still haven't found your key. Perhaps you ought to ask Gott or Himmell."

He obviously knew the names. His eyes narrowed and his mouth twitched as if he had just swallowed one of his poisoned corn pellets.

"We are looking for it, Mr. Fat Man," Herbert said. "And we'll let you know as soon as we've found it."

"I gave you two days." The Fat Man plucked the carnation out of his buttonhole and threw it into the grave. "You've run out of time." Then he turned his back on us and walked away.

I'd had enough. Coming to the funeral had been a mistake—a dead end in every sense of the word. We hadn't picked up anything apart, perhaps, from double pneumonia. And if it had been a chance to meet a few old friends, they were all old friends I'd have preferred to avoid. Herbert sneezed. "I need a shot of Scotch," he said for the benefit of the undertaker or anyone else who might be listening. I knew that once we got back to the apartment, he'd actually fix himself with a shot of cod-liver oil.

But I was wrong there. Things didn't turn out quite the way I expected.

We made a couple of stops on the way back. Herbert had

cashed the check and we had enough money to go wild and buy some Alka-Seltzer and another box of Maltesers.

"What do you want them for?" Herbert asked.

"I've got a headache," I said.

"No . . . the Maltesers."

So I explained. Whoever had snatched Lauren Bacardi might know by now that Johnny Naples had spent the last month of his life traipsing around London with a box of Maltesers. And they might come looking for them. The dwarf's box was still safely hidden underneath the floor. I'd bought the second box as a sort of insurance. I'd leave it somewhere nice and easy to find, just in case anyone else broke in.

We got back to the apartment and let ourselves in, dripping on the doormat. Maybe I noticed that the street door was unlocked when it wasn't supposed to be. Maybe I didn't. I don't remember. What with the rain, I was just glad to be in. We went upstairs. Herbert sneezed again. The office door was open and this time I did notice.

"Herbert," I said.

We went into the office. Herbert's eyes must have gone straight to the desk because he went and picked something up. "What's this doing here?" I heard him say.

But I didn't look at him. My eyes were on the corpse stretched out beneath the window. It took me a minute before I remembered where I'd seen him before, but I should have known from the moment I saw the chauffeur's uniform.

It was Lawrence, the Fat Man's driver. He was still wearing his one-way glasses, but one of the lenses had become a spiderweb of cracks, shattered by the bullet that had gone one way through it.

"Nick . . ." Herbert whimpered in a voice of pure jelly.

I looked up. And I saw it all.

"What's this doing here?" Herbert had asked. I replayed the words in my head. "This" was a gun. It had been lying on the carpet beside the desk. Now he was holding it. At that moment, the door opened. Snape and Boyle had followed us in. And there was me kneeling beside another dead man. There was Herbert, again, holding the gun that had just killed him. And there were the two policemen looking at us in open-mouthed astonishment.

"You're under—" Snape began.

"No . . ." Herbert moaned.

"I don't believe it," I said.

CROCODILE TEARS

Herbert and I spent the night back at the Ladbroke Grove Police Station. I'd never slept behind bars before—not that I got a lot of sleep that night either. There was a double bunk in our cell and I took the top level, with Herbert underneath. He'd caught a nasty cold in the cemetery, and every time I was about to drift away he'd let loose with a deafening sneeze and I'd be awake again. The bunk wasn't too comfortable either: just a narrow board with an inch-thick mattress, a sheet, and two blankets you could have struck a match on. I dropped off around midnight. Then I climbed back on and tried to get some sleep.

"Nick . . ." It could have been any time when Herbert's disembodied voice floated up out of the darkness.

"Yes?" I said.

"Are you awake?"

"No. I'm sleep-talking."

"Nick, I've been thinking." Herbert paused, sneezed, continued. "Maybe I'm not cut out to be a private detective after all."

"Whatever makes you think that, Herbert?" I asked.

"Well . . . I'm wanted for two murders, kidnapping, and disturbing the peace. The Fat Man wants to kill me. My apartment has been torn apart. And I haven't actually been able to detect anything."

"You may have a point," I agreed.

He sighed. "In the morning I'll tell Snape everything. He can have the Maltesers. I wish I'd given them to him in the first place."

That woke me up like a bucket of ice water. Five million dollars in diamonds and he wanted to give them away! I leaned over the side of the bunk. It was so dark that I couldn't see a thing, but I hoped that I was addressing Herbert's ear rather than his feet. "Herbert," I said. "If you whisper one word about those Maltesers, I will personally kill you."

"But, Nick—"

"No, Herbert. Those Maltesers are the only hope you've got."

"But . . . uh . . . uh . . ." He sneezed again. "But I might get sent to prison!" he protested.

"Don't worry," I said. "I'll visit you every Friday."

They woke us up at seven in the morning. We were allowed to wash and then a guard brought us each a mug of tea. I asked for a bacon sandwich, but all I got was a nasty look. Then it was back into the interrogation room—for Herbert but not for me. Snape stopped me at the door. Boyle was with him, growling softly. That was one guy I wanted to steer clear of. I wouldn't even have trusted Boyle to take my fingerprints. Not if I wanted to keep my fingers.

"You can go, laddie," Snape said. "It's only big brother we want."

"How long are you going to keep him for?" I asked. "It's only five days to Christmas."

"So?"

"He hasn't had time to buy my present yet."

Snape was unimpressed. "We'll keep him as long as it takes," he said. "I'll tell a social worker to visit you—to make sure you're all right."

"I'll visit him!" Boyle grunted.

"No, you won't, Boyle!" Snape rasped.

I jerked a thumb at the police assistant. "He needs a social worker more than me," I said.

Boyle lumbered a few steps toward me, but then Snape grabbed hold of him. For a minute it was as if I wasn't there.

"You're being ridiculous, Boyle," Snape muttered. "I've told you about those violent videos . . ."

"I just want to—" Boyle began.

"No! No! No! How many times do I have to tell you. This isn't the right sort of image for a modern metropolitan police force."

"It used to be," Boyle growled.

"In Transylvania," Snape replied. He turned back to me. "Go on, son. Out of here," he said. I glanced at Herbert, who sneezed miserably. The door slammed. And suddenly I was alone.

———

I didn't do much that morning. There wasn't much I could do. As I sat in Herbert's office with my feet up on his desk, I tried to work out who might have pulled the plug on the Fat Man's chauffeur and why. By midmorning I had it more or less figured out. It went like this: The Fat Man gives us two days to come up with the goods and we run out of time, so he decides to have a rummage around our apartment for himself. He sees us arriving at the Falcon's funeral and that gives him the chance he wants. While he holds us up in the cemetery—there was no other reason for the little chat we had—his faithful chauffeur and housebreaker, Lawrence, is turning the place over. At least, that's the plan.

But whoever kidnapped Lauren Bacardi (and my money's still on Gott and Himmell) has been asking her questions. She tells them about the box of Maltesers. So they nip back to pick them up and that's when they find Lawrence. Maybe there's a fight. Maybe they just didn't like him. Either way, they shoot him just before Herbert and I get back from the funeral. They make a hasty exit through the bathroom window and over the roof. We get left with the body.

Simple as that.

I opened the drawer of Herbert's desk. The box of Maltesers was still there—the fake box that I'd bought myself. The real box was still under the floorboard, covered in dust. I was just about to pull it out and have another look at it when the telephone rang.

"Hello?" It was a woman's voice. Soft, hesitant, perhaps foreign. I figured she must have the wrong number. I didn't know any soft, hesitant, perhaps foreign women. But then she asked, "Tim Diamond?"

"He's not here," I told her. "I'm his partner."

"His partner?"

"Yeah—but right now I'm working solo. How can I help you?"

There was a pause at the other end of the line. Then the lady made up her mind. "Can you come out . . . to Hampstead? I need to see you."

"Who is this?"

"Beatrice von Falkenberg."

That made me think. So the black widow had finally come crawling out of the woodwork—or to be more accurate, the telephone line. What did she want me for? "Suppose I'm busy . . ." I said.

"I'll make it worth your while."

"You'll pay for the train fare?"

"Take a taxi."

I agreed, so she gave me an address on the West Heath Road and told me to be there by twelve. I wondered if this was another decoy—if the moment I was gone somebody else would be elbowing their way into the flat. But so long as the fake Maltesers were in the desk, I figured I was covered. I changed my shirt and ran a comb through my hair. When I left, I was still a wreck, but at least I was a slightly tidier wreck. Once the widow discovered I was only thirteen years old, I didn't think she'd really care how I dressed.

I'd charge her for a taxi, but I took the subway to Hampstead and then walked. Hampstead, in case you don't know it, is in the north of London in the green belt. For "green," read "money." You don't have to be rich to live in Hampstead. You have to be loaded. It seemed to me that every other car I passed was a Rolls-Royce and even the garbage cans had burglar alarms. I got directions from a traffic cop and walked around the back of the village. A quarter of an hour later I arrived at the Falcon's lair.

It was a huge place, standing on a hill overlooking the Heath. Whoever said crime doesn't pay should have dropped by for an eyeful. It was the sort of house I'd have dreamed about—only I'd have had to take a mortgage out just to pay for the dream. Ten bedrooms? Eleven? It could have slept fifteen or more under those gabled roofs, and with the price of property in that part of town I figured forty winks would probably cost you ten bucks a wink. And that was just the top floor. Through the windows on the ground floor I could glimpse a kitchen as big as a dining room and a dining room as big as a swimming pool. There was a swimming pool, too, running along four windows to the right of the front door. Mind you, the way things were around here, that could have just been the bath.

I reached out and pressed the front doorbell. It went *bing-bong,* which was a bit of an anticlimax. After all that had gone before, I'd been expecting a massed choir. The door opened and there was another anticlimax. Beatrice von Falkenberg opened it herself. So what had happened to the butler? She looked at me with disinterest and mild distaste. I could see we were going to get along fine.

"Yes?" she asked.

"I'm Nick," I said. "Nick Diamond. You asked me to come here."

"Did I?" She shrugged. "I was expecting someone older."

"Well . . . I can come back in twenty years, if you like."

"No, no . . . come in."

I followed her in, suddenly feeling like a scruffy chimney sweep. She was young for a widow; maybe about forty, with black hair clinging to her head like a bathing cap. Her skin was pale, her lips a kiss of dark red. She was wearing some sort of housedress with a slit all the way up to her waist and she moved like she had never left the stage—not walking but flowing. Everything about her spelled class. The slim, crystal champagne glass in one hand. Even the tin plate with the lumps of raw meat in the other.

"I was about to feed my pet," she explained.

"Dog?" I asked.

She glanced at the plate. "No. I think it's beef."

We'd gone into the room with the swimming pool. It had been designed so that you could sit around it in bamboo chairs sipping cocktails from the bar at the far end, watching the guests swim. Only there were no bamboo chairs, the bar was empty, and I was the only guest. I looked around and suddenly realized that although I was in a millionaire's house, the millions had long gone. There was no furniture. Faded patches on the walls showed where the pictures had once been. The curtain rods had lost their curtains. Even the potted plants were dead. The house was a shell. All it contained was a widow in a housedress with a glass of champagne and a tin of raw meat.

"Fido!" she called out. "Come on, darling!"

Something splashed in the water. I swallowed. Apart from the widow in the housedress with the champagne and the tin of raw meat, it seemed that the house also contained an alligator. The last time I had seen an alligator it was hanging on some rich woman's arm with lipsticks and credit cards inside. But this one was no handbag. It was very alive, waddling out of the pool, its ugly black eyes fixed on the plate of meat.

"Don't worry," the widow said. "He's very fond of strangers."

"Yeah—cooked or raw?" I asked.

She smiled and tossed Fido a piece of meat. Its great jaws snapped shut and it made a horrid gulping sound as its throat bulged, sucking the meat down. She held up a second piece. "I want the Maltesers," she said.

"Maltesers?"

She threw the piece of meat, but this time she made sure that it fell short so the creature had to stalk forward to get it. It stalked forward toward me. "They belonged to my husband," she went on. "The dwarf stole them; I want them back."

I pointed at the alligator. It was getting too close for comfort. As far as I was concerned, a hundred miles would have been too close for comfort. "Do you have a permit for that thing?" I asked.

"I don't know," she said. "It was a present from my late husband."

"Have you ever thought about pussycats?"

"Fido ate the pussycats."

I thought of turning and running, but I couldn't be sure I'd make it to the door. The alligator had short, wrinkled legs, but at the moment I can't say mine felt much better. It was only a few feet or so away. Its black eyes were fixed on me, almost daring me to make a move. The whole thing was crazy. I'd never been threatened by an alligator before.

"I don't have the Maltesers," I said. "Tim has them."

"And where is he?"

"In jail . . . Ladbroke Grove Police Station."

She paused for a long minute and looked at me with cold eyes. The eyes burrowed into me, trying to work out if I was telling the truth. In the end they must have believed me because she laughed and threw the rest of the meat into the swimming pool. The alligator corkscrewed around and dived after it.

"I like you," she said. "You're not afraid." She walked over to me and put an arm around my shoulders. She hadn't managed to frighten me, so now she was trying to charm me. She wouldn't manage that either. Given a choice, I'd have preferred to spend time with the alligator.

"When Henry von Falkenberg died," she said, "all his money went with him. This house isn't mine, Nick. I've had to sell the contents just to pay the rent. Even Fido is going to the zoo. It breaks my heart, but I can't afford to keep him. And now I don't have a friend in the world." There were tears in her eyes. Crocodile tears, I thought. Or alligator. "There is only one hope for me, Nicholas. The Maltesers. Henry wanted me to have them. They belong to me."

"What's so special about them?" I asked.

"To you—nothing," she replied. "But to me . . . They're worth five hundred dollars if you'll get them back for me. That's how much I'll pay you."

"I thought you had no money."

"I'll find it. Maybe Fido will end up as suitcases after all." She walked me back to the door and opened it.

"Talk to Herbert," she said. "When the police release him, bring the Maltesers here. I will have the money, I swear it. And to you they are useless. You must see that."

"What about my taxi fare home?" I asked.

"When you come with the Maltesers . . ." She shut the door.

"See you later, alligator," I muttered.

So that was Beatrice von Falkenberg! A strange, lonely woman, sharing her memories with a strange, lonely pet. I walked back down the road toward Hampstead, and as I went I turned over two questions in my mind. If the Falcon had been so secretive, how come she had found out about the Maltesers? It seemed unlikely that he had told her. So who had?

The second thing was even stranger. She had telephoned me and asked to speak to Tim Diamond. I hadn't said anything on the subject of my brother. So how had she known that his real name was Herbert?

KILLER IN THE RAIN

I didn't go back to the flat that afternoon. It wouldn't have been the same without Herbert. Quieter, tidier, less danger- ous, and generally nicer . . . but not the same. Also I was wor- ried about him. I wouldn't want to spend half an hour with Snape and Boyle, let alone a whole day. Boyle could have killed him by now. On the other hand, if Herbert told them about the Maltesers, I'd kill him myself. Either way he was in big trouble, and the sooner I found out just what was go- ing on, the better it would be for him.

Things might have been different if Lauren Bacardi had been able to tell me where the dwarf had been when he worked out what the Maltesers meant. If I could see what he had seen, maybe I'd be able to work it out, too. But I had a nasty feeling that the only way I'd be able to talk to Lauren again would be with a Ouija board. The people who had snatched her were playing for keeps. By now she probably had more lead in her than a church roof.

That just left the dwarf. Johnny Naples might be pushing up the daisies himself, but if I could pick up his trail I might still learn something. His book of matches had led me to Lauren Bacardi. I wondered what else I might find in his room. So that afternoon I took the subway to Notting Hill and walked back down the Portobello Road to the Hotel Splendide.

I passed Hammett's newsstand on the way. The old guy who owned it was standing in the window and he saw me pass. I'm only guessing now, but I suppose he must have picked up the telephone and called the hotel a moment later. And at the hotel, Jack Splendide must have made a phone call of his own. Like I say, I'm only guessing. But it took me ten minutes to walk from the newsstand to the hotel and that was just about all the time they needed to arrange my death.

The hotel was just like I remembered it, leaning carelessly against the overpass. The plainclothes policeman and the dog had gone, of course, but the garbage cans were still there, spitting their leftovers into the gutter. It was after three and already it was getting dark, the sun sliding behind the horizon like a drunk behind a bar. An old man carrying two plastic bags full of junk stumbled past, on his way from one nowhere to another. A cold wind scattered the litter across the street. Depressing? Well, it was five days to Christmas and I was pretty depressed myself.

I went into the hotel. Jack Splendide was sitting behind the counter where I'd found him on my first visit. He was reading a dirty paperback. It was so dirty, you couldn't read half the words. It looked like somebody had spilled their breakfast all over it. He was still sucking a cigar—probably the same cigar, and he hadn't changed his shirt either. The last time he'd changed that shirt I probably hadn't been born.

"Hello," I said.

"Yeah?" He really knew how to make a guy feel welcome.

"I want a room."

"How long for?"

"One hour."

He frowned. "We only rent by the night. Fifteen dollars. Sixteen dollars with a bed."

I'd managed to grab all Herbert's cash before we parted company and now I counted out the money on the counter. Splendide took it, then stood up, reaching for the key.

"I want Room thirty-nine," I said.

"Suppose it's taken?"

I gestured at the hooks. "The key's there," I said. "Anyway—who needs it? The room doesn't have a lock."

"This is a class hotel, kid." He was offended. The cigar waggled between his teeth like a finger ticking me off. "You don't like it, you can check in someplace else."

I didn't like it. But I had to go through with it. "Just give me the key," I said.

He argued a bit more after that. I thought he was holding out for more money, but of course he was keeping me waiting on purpose. That was what he had been told to do. In the end he let me have the key—like he'd been intending to all the time. I should have been smart enough to see right through his little act, but it had been a long day and I was tired and . . . okay, maybe I wasn't as smart as I thought.

Anyway, he gave me the key and I climbed up the stairs to

the fifth floor, then along the corridor to Room 39. It was only when I'd opened the door and gone in that I began to think that maybe this wasn't such a good idea after all. It was unlikely that the room had been cleaned since the dwarf's death—it was unlikely that the rooms at the Hotel Splendide were ever cleaned—but the police would have been through it with a fine-tooth comb. But now that I was here, it wouldn't hurt to have a look. And I had paid.

I began with the drawers. There was a big, asthmatic chest of them. They groaned when I pulled them open and the brass rings rattled. But apart from a bent safety pin, a moth-ball, and the moth it had killed, they were empty. Next I tried the table. That should have had two more drawers, but somebody had stolen them. That just left the bed. I went and sat on it, remembering how Johnny Naples had lain there with that red carnation blossoming in the buttonhole of his shirt. He had sat in this room. He had lived in it. He had worked out the location of a five-million-dollar fortune in it. And he had died in it.

The traffic thundered past about six feet away from the window. It was still a mystery how Johnny Naples had ever managed to sleep here at all.

My eye was drawn to a wastepaper basket in one corner. It was a green plastic thing, so broken and battered that it should have been in a wastebasket itself. I leaned across and flicked a hand through the rubbish that lay in the bottom. There wasn't much: two potato-chip bags, the wrapper from a chocolate bar, a couple of dead batteries, and an empty pack of cigarettes. I was about to leave it when I remembered. It wouldn't have meant anything to the police—that was why they'd overlooked it—but it meant something to me. Back in the office, the day it had all started, the dwarf had smoked Turkish cigarettes. And this was a Turkish cigarette pack. It had belonged to Naples.

I plucked it out of the wastepaper basket and opened it, hoping . . . I don't know . . . for a telephone number scrawled on the inside or something like that. What I got was even better. It was a shower of paper: little white squares that had been neatly torn up. I knelt down and examined the scraps. Some of them had writing on them, parts of words written in blue ink. I slid them across the carpet with a pointed finger, putting the jigsaw puzzle back together again. It didn't take me long before I had it: five words in English with what I guessed were the Spanish translations written beside them.

DIGITAL

PHOTODETECTOR

LIGHT-EMITTING DIODE

Frankly, they were a disappointment. Why had Johnny Naples written them down? I was certain they had to be connected with the Maltesers. That would explain why, after he'd torn the paper up, he'd taken the extra precaution of hiding them in the cigarette pack. He'd have flushed them down the toilet if the hotel had toilets. It was the Spanish translations that helped me figure it out. Suppose Johnny Naples had come across the five words in his search for the diamonds. His English was good, but it wasn't that good. He might not have understood them. So he'd have written them down to look up later.

The only snag was, I didn't understand them either. Obviously, they were something to do with science, but science had never been my strong point. If you met my science teacher, I think you'd know why. I don't think science was his strong point either.

I scooped the pieces up and put them in my pocket. I'd searched the drawers, the table, and the wastepaper basket. That left just the bed. I tried to look underneath it, but a wooden rim running down to the carpet made that impossible. It was one of the oldest beds I had ever seen, a monster of thick wood and rusty springs with a mattress a foot and a half thick and about as comfortable as a damp sponge cake. It took all my strength to heave the thing up on its side, but I was determined to look underneath. Not that there was much to discover: a yellowed copy of the *Daily Mirror,* one slipper, and about ten years' worth of accumulated dust.

But it was the bed that saved my life.

I was just about to set it down when I heard the window shatter and at the same time a car roared away.

Something dark green and about the size of a softball had flown into the room. It took me about one second to work out that it wasn't a dark green softball and another second to throw myself to the ground. The grenade hit the bed and bounced back toward the window. Then it exploded.

I should have been killed, but I was already hugging the floor and there was this great wall of springs and mattress between me and it. Even so it was like being inside a cherry bomb on New Year's Eve. Suddenly it seemed that the whole room was on fire—not just the room, the very air in the room. The floor buckled upward like a huge fist, pounding me in the stomach. The explosion was so loud I thought it would crack open my skull. All this happened at once, and at the same time I was seized by the shock wave and hurled back, twisting in the air, and finally thrown out of the room, my shoulders slamming into the door and carrying it with me. I was unconscious by the time I hit the floor. I don't know how long I stayed like that. Maybe ten minutes. It could have been ten days.

I woke up with a mouth full of splinters and two hysterical opera singers screaming in my ears. Actually, there weren't any opera singers, but that's what it sounded like. My clothes were torn to ribbons and I could feel the blood running from a cut above one eye. Other than that, I seemed to be in remarkably good health for someone who had just been blown up. There would be plenty of bruises, but there were no broken bones. I stood up—one bone at a time—and leaned against a wall for support. The wall slid away. There was too much dust and smoke in the air to see. I stood where

I was, waiting for things to settle down a bit before I made any sudden move.

Which was just as well. The Hotel Splendide had been waiting for an excuse to fall down for twenty years or more. The grenade had been all it needed. The whole of the back wall, the one that faced the overpass, had simply collapsed and I was now standing on a piece of floor that stretched into thin air. I shivered as the breeze whipped the smoke up around me. The traffic roared past, a blur of brightly colored metal whirling endlessly into the night. I was surprised that nobody had stopped . . . but how could they? It was an overpass. Doubtless the police would shut it down soon enough, but anyone stopping right now would only add a multiple pileup to the evening's entertainment.

I stepped back, looking for the staircase or whatever might be left of it. This looked like it would be the hotel's last night. The hotel, what was left of it, was on fire, the flames spreading rapidly, the wood snapping, water hissing out of broken pipes. My hearing still wasn't back to normal, but I could just about make out the sound of people shouting. In the distance, police cars or fire engines or something with sirens were drawing nearer. A naked man ran past, his face half covered in shaving foam. I followed him. We'd both had a close shave that day.

My guardian angel must have been working overtime just then. Lucky it didn't belong to a trade union. The iron bar narrowly missed my head and I didn't even notice it until it smashed into the wall, spraying me with plaster. I wheeled around and there was Jack Splendide, lifting the bar to try his luck again. His shirt was in shreds and his stomach wasn't a whole lot better. Both his trouser legs had been blown off at the knee. I realized he must have been close to the dwarf's room when the explosion happened—perhaps in the room next door. And he didn't seem too happy that I'd survived.

He swung the bar again and this time I dodged. He was about forty pounds overweight and that made him slow. On the other hand, he didn't need to be too fast. He was between me and the staircase. I had the flames on one side of me and a five-story fall right behind me. I wondered if I could jump across onto the overpass. It was only about six feet, but the way I was feeling right then it was about three feet too far. I leaped back, avoiding a third blow. Now I was in the ruins of what had been Room 39. The flames were getting nearer. So was Jack Splendide.

He was shouting at me. What with all the din and the screaming in my ears, it was difficult to make out what he was saying, but I gathered that he blamed me for the destruction of his hotel. He must have really liked that place. There were tears running down his cheeks and he was holding that iron bar (part of a towel rail) with genuine affection. I wanted to explain that it wasn't my fault that a passing motorist had decided to hurl a bomb at me, but he wouldn't listen to reason. Jack Splendide had flipped. And he wanted me dead.

The iron bar came curving up over his shoulder as he swung it with both hands, but then the top got snarled up in a loop of wire. As it came down, it tore the wire out of the wall and for a few seconds electric sparks danced in the air. That distracted him just long enough for me to grab hold of a piece of table and bring it crashing into his stomach. He howled and dropped the bar. I hit him again, this time propelling him forward right to the edge of the floor.

He flailed at the air with his hands. There was a fall of at least forty feet to the cold, hard concrete below and I thought that was just where he was heading. Unable to regain his balance, he yelled and plunged forward, his body lunging out into the night. But at the last moment he managed to grab hold of the very edge of the overpass. And that was how he finished up: a human bridge. His feet were on the floor in what was left of Room 39. His hands were desperately clutching a piece of metal jutting out of the side of the overpass. His body sagged between the two.

I looked behind me. The flames were closing in. I wouldn't even make it through the shattered doorway now. But I wasn't too keen on jumping across to the overpass. Jack Splendide was the only answer. A human bridge. I took two big steps. One foot in the small of his back and I was across—safely standing on the edge of the road.

"Kid . . . hey, kid!" I heard him and walked back over to him. He was a big, strong man, but he couldn't stay like that much longer. "Help me!" he rasped, the sweat dripping off his forehead. The wind jerked at my shirt. The cars roared by, only inches away now. Some of the drivers honked at me, but they couldn't see Jack Splendide. I crouched down close to him. By now I'd been able to put a few things together.

"Who was it, Splendide?" I asked. "Who threw the grenade?"

"Please!" His hands tightened their hold as his body swayed.

"You must have told them I was here. Who was it?"

There was no way he could stall me. He was getting weaker by the minute and across the gap the flames were creeping up on him. He could probably feel them with the soles of his feet. "It was the Fat Man," he gasped. "He guessed you might go back to the hotel. He paid me . . . to call if you did."

"Why?"

"You insulted him, kid. Nobody insults the Fat Man. But I didn't know he was going to try and kill you. I mean . . . the grenade. Honest, kid. I thought he was just going to take a shot at you—to scare you."

Yeah, I thought. And you came up to the fifth floor to watch.

"Help me!" he whimpered. "Give me a hand, kid. I can't hold on much longer."

"That's true," I said, straightening up.

"You can't leave me here, kid. You can't!"

"Wanna bet?"

I walked away, leaving him stretched out between the flames and the overpass with a long, long way to fall if he let go. Maybe the police or firemen reached him in the end. To be honest, I don't really care. Jack Splendide had set me up to be killed. He might not have been expecting a grenade, but he'd known the Fat Man didn't play games.

It had begun to rain. Pulling the remains of my shirt closer to my shivering skin, I walked down the overpass and forgot about him.

THE PROFESSOR

I was woken by the smell of lavender. Lavender? Yes—
perfume. You've smelled it before, Nick. Where? I can't remember, but maybe it was mixed with the raw meat and . . .
I swallowed, stretched, opened my eyes.

"Blimey, you're a sight!" Betty Charlady exclaimed.

I was half stretched out on Herbert's desk in his office. I'd
had to walk home the night before, and by the time I'd gotten in I'd been too tired to go upstairs. I'd looked at the second flight of steps. They led to a bed with a crumpled sheet
and a tangled-up quilt. I'll never make it, I'd thought, and so
I'd gone into the office and collapsed there. And now Betty
Charlady was standing in front of me, looking at me like I'd
dropped in from another planet.

"What happened to you?" she demanded, shaking her
head and sending the artificial daisies on her hat into convulsions.

"I had a bad night," I said. "How did you get in?"

"Through the door."

"It was open?"

She nodded. "You ought to lock it at night, Master
Nicholas. You never know who might visit . . ."

I needed a hot bath, a hot meal, two aspirin, and a warm

bed—not necessarily in that order. Instead I went up and washed my face in the sink while Betty made breakfast: boiled eggs, toast, and coffee. I looked at myself in the mirror. Somebody else looked back. His hair was a mess, there were bags under his eyes, and he had a nasty cut on his forehead. I felt sorry for the guy.

Ten minutes later, I was sitting down in the kitchen, eating. Betty had insisted on cutting my toast into triangles, which was pretty embarrassing. I'd been threatened, blown up, attacked—and here I was being treated like a kid again. But I suppose she meant well.

"Where's Mr. Timothy?" she asked.

"Herbert?" I said. "He's in jail. Accused of murder."

"Murder!" she shrieked. "That's a crime!"

"Well . . . yes."

"No. I mean accusing Mr. Herbert of doing anything like that." She sniffed. "Anybody could see he wouldn't hurt a fly."

She was right there. Herbert ran away from flies. He was probably the only private detective in the country who was even scared of goldfish.

"So you're doing all the detective work for him," she said. I nodded. "Have you found anything out yet?"

Had I found anything out? Well, I'd found out that Beatrice von Falkenberg had strange taste in pets. I'd found out that if you stood too close to an exploding grenade, it made your ears hurt. I'd found out that the Fat Man still wanted to lose weight and that I was the weight he wanted to lose. But when you added up everything I'd found out, it would just about fit on the back of a postage stamp and you wouldn't even need to write in small letters.

"No, Betty," I said. "I haven't found anything out. Not unless you know what a digital detector or a photo lighter is."

"A wot?" she asked.

The scraps of paper that I had found in the dwarf's room were still safely in my shirt pocket. The trouble was, my shirt pocket was still in the hotel. It had been blown off the shirt by the blast and for the life of me I couldn't remember exactly what the words had been.

"I'm going to have a bath," I said.

"I'll run it for you," Betty volunteered.

I shook my head. Any more encouragement and she'd be offering to scrub my back. "No, thanks . . . you go home. I can manage."

"But what about the cleaning?"

I reached into my pocket and pulled out one of Herbert's ten-dollar bills. It hurt me to see it go, but there was no denying that Betty had done a good job. When she'd come, the flat had looked like a junkyard. Now it was more like an industrial slum. "Here you are," I said. "Come back next week, after Christmas."

"Ooh! Ta!" She took it. "Merry Christmas, Master Nicholas," she burbled.

"Merry Christmas, Betty," I said.

———

Sometime later, the doorbell dragged me out of a beautiful sleep. I looked at my watch. It said five to ten. It had said five to ten when I'd gone to bed. Either it had been a short sleep or I needed a new watch. I held it up to my ear and shook it. There was a dull *ping* and the second hand fell off. Well, that's what comes of buying a secondhand watch.

I pulled on a pair of jeans and a sweater and made my way downstairs. The bell was still ringing. Whoever was down there was leaning on the button. I pressed the intercom to let him in, hoping he wouldn't do the same to me. I don't like being leaned on, and in the last few days I'd had more than enough of it. I went into the office and had just sat down when my client walked in.

Correction—he didn't walk, he staggered. And I smelled him before I saw him. It must have been around lunchtime, but he'd been drinking since breakfast and he'd brought the stale reek of whiskey as his calling card.

I recognized him from somewhere. He was around sixty, small, fat, unshaven, owlish, with round glasses, dressed in a crumpled gray raincoat with bottle-size pockets.

He fumbled his way toward one of the chairs that Betty Charlady had repaired for us and sat down heavily, stretching out his legs. He was wearing green socks. I could see them through the holes in the soles of his shoes. I waited for him to say something, but he wasn't in a hurry. He pulled a single cigarette out of his pocket, straightened it between his thumb and forefinger, and twisted it into his mouth. He lit it with a trembling hand. The match had almost burned itself out before he found the end of the cigarette. He wasn't just a drunk. He was a nearsighted drunk. Suddenly I remembered where I'd seen him. He'd been at the Falcon's funeral, standing—swaying—next to Beatrice von Falkenberg.

"It's good to sit down," he said.

"You tired?" I asked.

"No. It's just that I keep falling over when I stand up. Or bumping into things." He sucked in smoke. "You see, sir, I got this problem . . ."

"Drink?" I muttered sympathetically.

"Thanks. I'll have a large Scotch."

I shook my head and slid an ashtray toward him. He flicked the cigarette and scattered ashes across the top of the desk. "Who are you?" I asked.

"The name's Quisling," he said. "Quentin Quisling."

"Your parents liked Qs," I said.

"Yeah—bus queues, shopping queues . . . but that's not why I'm here. You may have heard of me, sir. I used to be called the Professor."

Sure I'd heard of the Professor. That had been another of the names on Snape's blackboard. What had Snape told me? The Professor had been the Falcon's tame scientist, something of a whiz-kid. But a year ago he'd gone missing. Looking at him now, I could see where he'd been. On the skids. Professor Quisling might have been smart once, but now he looked like a scarecrow grown old and sick. He had the skin of a five-year-old cheese and he spoke with a wheezy, grating voice. He puffed smoke into the air and coughed. Cigarettes were killing him while booze was arranging the funeral.

"I wanted to see your brother," he said.

"He's not here."

"I can see that, sir. I don't see much. But I can see that." He pulled a half bottle of whiskey out of his pocket, unscrewed it, squinted, and tilted it toward his throat. The liquid ran down the side of his neck. He groped for the cigarette and found it. "All right," he said. "I'll split it with you. Fifty-fifty."

"The cigarette?" I asked.

"That's very funny, sir. I can see you have a sense of humor." He screwed the cigarette between his lips and coughed. It was a horrible cough. I could hear marbles rattling in his lungs. "You know who I am?" he asked.

"You just told me."

"I used to be the Falcon's brains." He stabbed at his chest with a bent thumb. "He wanted something fixed, I fixed it."

"Lightbulbs?" I asked.

"Oh no, sir. I invented things for him. Things you wouldn't understand."

"So what happened to you?" I asked.

"This happened to me." He waved the bottle. "But I know what you've got, sir. Indeed I do. I saw you at the funeral and

I figured it out. A packet of Maltesers, would it be? Well . . .
I know what to do with them. Together we could make
money."

"What are you suggesting, Professor?" I said.

"You give them to me and you wait here." He smiled at
me with crooked, sly eyes. "I'll come back tomorrow with half
the money."

I nodded, pretending to consider the offer. In fact I was
amazed. Here was a guy who was killing himself as sure as if
he had a noose around his neck. He couldn't afford a decent
pair of shoes and he was dressed like a dummy in a thrift
shop. But he thought he could pull a fast one on me just because I was a kid and he was a so-called adult. For a moment
he reminded me of my math teacher. You know the sort. Just
because they can work out the angles in an isosceles triangle,
they think they rule the world. I decided to string him along.

"I give you the Maltesers," I said. "And you come back
with half the loot?"

"That's right, sir," Quisling said. He finished the half
bottle and lobbed it toward the wastebasket. It missed and
smashed against the wall. He didn't seem to notice.

"But what do the Maltesers do?" I asked.

"They open the—" He stopped himself just in time. "I'll
tell you when I bring the money," he said.

I knew that once I'd given him the Maltesers I'd never see
him again. But I'd had an idea. I pulled open the drawer of
the desk and took out the box that I'd hidden there a few days

before. "This is what you want," I said. He reached forward hungrily, but I didn't let go. "You will come back?" I queried Quentin Quisling.

"Sure, sir. I'll come back. On my mother's grave."

The old girl probably wasn't even dead. "When?" I asked.

"Tomorrow morning," he said.

I lifted my hand and he snatched the box away.

"In the morning," he repeated.

The door slammed shut behind him.

I waited thirty seconds before I followed him. He wouldn't see me behind him. With his eyesight he wouldn't see me if I stood next to him. And if Quisling really did know where the Falcon's diamonds were hidden, he would lead me to them. The box of Maltesers I'd given him would, of course, be useless. But perhaps I'd let him keep them—after he'd led me to the end of the rainbow. That was the way I'd planned it, but of course that was far too easy, and when nothing can go wrong that's when everything always does. I'd reached the front door. I'd turned around to lock it behind me. I could hear an engine turning over—a van parked close by. There was a movement in the street. I glanced up just in time to see something short and unpleasant come thudding down. It hit me behind the ear. I was out like a light.

FAIRY CAKES

I wish somebody had told me it was Knock Out Nick Diamond Week in London. It had happened to me twice in two days and I was getting a bit tired of it. Being knocked out isn't so bad. It's waking up that's the real problem. Your head hurts, your mouth is dry, and you feel sick. And if it's pitch-dark and you're locked up in the back of a van that could be going anywhere, it's pretty scary, too.

I was still in London. I could tell from the sound of the traffic and from the number of times we stopped. Once—when we were at a traffic light or something—I heard vague voices outside and thought of hammering on the side of the van. But it probably wouldn't have done any good, and anyway, by the time I'd made up my mind, the van had moved off. A few minutes later, we stopped again. The door was pulled open. There wasn't a lot of light left in the day, but what there was of it streamed in and punched me in the eyes.

"Get out," a voice said. It was a soft voice, the sort of voice you'd expect to float on the scent of violets. It had a slight German twang. I'd heard that voice once before.

I got out.

The first thing I saw was a road sign. It read: BAYLY STREET SE1, which put me somewhere on the south bank of the river, opposite the financial district. I looked around me. This was warehouse territory. The old brick buildings rose five stories high on both sides of the road, the narrow gap of sky in between crisscrossed by corrugated iron walkways, hooks and chains, pipes and loading platforms. A hundred years ago, Bayly Street would have been on its feet. Twisted fuel cans, broken roof tiles, and yards of multicolored cables spilled out of the deserted buildings like entrails. The street was pitted with puddles that seemed to be eating their way into the carcass.

Another sign caught my eye, bright red letters on white: McAlpine. It was a death warrant in one word for Bayly Street. There's nothing more destructive than a construction company. They'd gut the warehouses and build fancy apartments in the shell. Each one would have a river view, a quarry-tiled garage, and a five-figure price tag. That's the trouble with London. The rich have got it all.

There was a man standing beside the van, holding a silenced gun that he was pointing in my direction. He might have been a gangster, but he went to a smart tailor. He was dressed in a pale gray suit with a pink tie. His shoes were as brightly polished as his smile. A moment later, the driver's door opened and a second man got out. He was dressed identically to the first, except that his tie was a powder blue. They were both short and thin and both wore their hair parted down the middle—one dark, one blond. They were both approaching fifty and had spent a lot of money trying to back away again. Their slightly plastic faces had to be the work of a slight plastic surgeon. Know what I mean? Cut out the fat, take up the wrinkles, retone the flesh, thank you, sir, and make sure you don't sneeze too violently.

"This way," Blondie said, gesturing with the gun.

"After you," I replied.

"I don't think so."

There had to be men at work on a construction site nearby. I could hear them now, their hydraulic drills jabbering away in the distance, the mechanical grabbers churning up the mud. I thought of making a break for it. But there was no chance. There was nobody in sight and they'd have shot me down before I'd gone ten feet. The driver had walked across to a heavy wooden door and unlocked a padlock the size of a soup plate. It led into a room like an abandoned garage: bare concrete floor, burned-out walls, junk everywhere. For a nasty minute I thought that this was it and that I was about to reach the last full stop, but there was a staircase in one corner and Blondie steered me toward it. We went up five flights. Each floor was the same—derelict and decaying. But then we came to another door and another padlock. The fifth floor was different.

It was a single, undivided space and about as big as a tennis court, only it would be difficult to have a game—not with a grand piano parked in the middle. It had a large, wide window—more like a French door really—reaching from floor to ceiling, but being five stories up, it didn't lead any-where. The room was furnished with a gray carpet, gray silk curtains, and a silvery three-piece suite arranged around a white marble table. There was an unpatitioned-off kitchen with a tray loaded with cups and plates for tea.

The dark-haired man went into the kitchen while Blondie waved me over to the sofa.

"And who are you?" I asked, although I already had a good idea.

"I'm William," Blondie said. "And that's Eric." He ges-tured.

"Gott and Himmell," I muttered. The two German schoolboys from Eton. That gave me a complete score on Snape's blackboard.

"We thought it was time we invited you to tea," Gott went on. "I do hope you like fairy cakes."

The kettle boiled. Himmell filled the pot and brought the tray over to the table. "Who's going to be mother?" I asked. They both raised their eyebrows at that. I couldn't believe it. These were meant to be the Falcon's two right-hand men, but they looked about as dangerous as my two maiden aunts. But then I remembered the way they'd brought me here and the fact that there were two dead bodies to be accounted for. They might look like a joke. But they could still make you die laughing.

Himmell poured the tea into china cups decorated with

roses interlaced with swastikas, and then handed out the fairy cakes. I didn't feel like eating, but it looked like he'd made them himself and I didn't want to hurt his feelings.

"Who plays the piano?" I asked. Polite conversation seemed like a good idea.

"We both do," Gott said. "But now, my friend, it's your turn to sing." Himmell laughed at that. I didn't. I've found funnier lines in a Latin dictionary. "You have something we want," Gott went on. "Let me explain, Nicholas . . . if I may call you Nicholas? A charming name."

I bit into the fairy cake. It tasted like dish soap.

"We were following the dwarf the day he visited you and your brother. We didn't know then what he was carrying. We searched your apartment that evening, but we found nothing. Then we ran into Miss Bacardi."

"Is she here?" I asked.

"You'll see her soon enough. She told us about the Maltesers. Most . . . unusual. So we went back to your flat for a second time. That was the day of the Falcon's funeral. We were certain that we would find the Maltesers then. But after we'd broken in, we were surprised. Who was the man waiting for us?"

"His name was Lawrence," I said. "He was the chauffeur of the Fat Man. He was after the Maltesers, too."

"It was unfortunate for him." Gott sighed. "He said some very hurtful things. So Eric hurt him. In fact, he killed him. I have to tell you, Nicholas. Eric is a lovely person. Lovely.

But he gets moody sometimes. And when he's moody, he shoots people."

I smiled at Himmell. "Nice fairy cakes," I said.

"We still want the Maltesers," Gott said. "We know your brother is in jail. And we know you know where they are. So either you tell us now or . . ."

"Or what, Gott?" I asked.

"It would be a terrible shame," he replied. "You're a very nice boy. Really very sweet. How old are you?"

"Thirteen."

"Yes—far too young to end up in a plastic bag with six bullets in your chest. Would you like some more tea?"

Himmell filled my cup. He didn't seem to have quite as good a grasp of the English language as his friend. They were both still smiling at me with their plastic smiles and I wondered if, after the face-lifts, they were capable of anything else. Gott finished his tea and smacked his lips.

"Thank you," he said. "You do make a lovely cup, Eric."

"Anudder cup?"

"*Nein danke.*" He turned to me. "So where are they?"

I'd been thinking. I'd have been happy to tell them if I thought it would get me out of there. But somehow I didn't believe it. Once they'd gotten what they wanted, they wouldn't need me and I'd be in that plastic bag like a shot. And I mean shot. I had to buy time. Given a bit of time, maybe I could find my way out of this jam.

I coughed. "Well, it's a bit tricky . . ." Himmell's face fell.

He was still smiling, but I figure his nose and chin must have sunk a good half inch or so. "I mean, I do have them. They're at Victoria Station. In a luggage locker. But Herbert has the key."

"The number?"

"Um . . . one hundred and eighty!" I'd been making it up as I went along and I sang out that number like an auctioneer after a final bid.

"At Victoria Station?"

"Yes. But you can't open it."

He lifted the gun. "I think we can."

Gott got to his feet and strolled over to the piano. Then he sat down on the stool and rubbed his hands over the keys. I stood up. "Thanks for the tea," I said. "If that's all you wanted to know—"

"You're not going anywhere." Gott played a chord. "Eric!"

Himmell had a few cords of his own. I don't know where he'd gotten the rope from, but there was nothing I could do. While Gott played a tune on the piano Himmell tied me up. He did it very professionally. My hands went behind my back, where they were introduced to my feet. By the time he'd finished, I couldn't even twitch in time to the music and I could feel my fingers and toes going blue as the blood was cut off. Gott finished his little recital and stood up.

"Well, Nicholas," he said. "We're going to Victoria Station." He looked at his watch. "We'll be back around five. And if you've been lying, we'll bury you around five-thirty."

I tried to shrug. I couldn't even manage that with all the ropes. "If this is what they teach you at private school," I said, "I'm glad I went public."

"Take him into the back room," Gott snapped. "It's time he met our other guest."

Himmell picked me up and carried me across the room. I'm not heavy, but he was still stronger than I thought. There was a door at the far end, beyond the piano. He drew back a metal bolt with one hand and opened it.

"When are you going to let me out of here?" a voice demanded. A voice I knew.

Himmell threw me down on the floor. I found myself sitting opposite Lauren Bacardi. She was tied up just like me.

"Company for you," Gott said.

He closed the door and locked it behind him. A minute later I heard the two Germans leave for Victoria Station. I wondered what they'd find in Locker 180. I wondered if there even *was* a Locker 180. I just knew that I had until five to get out of here. I'd bought myself time okay. But I wasn't too keen on paying the price.

With an effort, I tried to put them out of my mind. I looked around at Lauren. "Hi," I said.

"I know you," she said.

"Yeah. Nick Diamond. We met at the Casablanca Club— the night they came for you."

She nodded. "I remember. Thanks a bunch, Nick. I was enjoying my life until you came along."

She was still dressed in the glitzy clothes she had worn for her singing act, but the fake jewelry was gone and she had washed off some of the makeup. She looked better without it. She was sitting in the corner with her knees drawn up, a plate and a mug on the floor beside her. There was no furniture in the room, which was about as big as a large walk-in closet. It was lit by a single small window that would have been too high up to reach even if we hadn't been tied up. I gave a cautious tug at the ropes. In the movies, there would have been a piece of broken glass or something for me to cut them with. But it looked like I was in the wrong movie.

I gave up. "I'm sorry about this," I said. "But I didn't lead them to you."

"No? Then who did?"

It was a good question. How had they found out about her? "You told them about the Maltesers?" I said.

She sniffed. "Why else do you think I'm still alive?"

"Enjoy it while you can," I said. "They're going to be back at five and they're not going to be very happy. I strung them a line out there. When they get back, I reckon they're going to want to string me up with one."

"Then we'd better move."

"Sure. If I can just get across to you, maybe you can get at my ropes with your teeth and—"

I stopped. Lauren Bacardi had wriggled. That was all she had done, but now the ropes were falling away from her like overcooked spaghetti. It was incredible. I tried it myself. But while she got to her feet, unhooking the last loop from her wrist, I stayed exactly where I was.

"That's a real trick," I said. "How did you do it?"

"Before I became a singer I worked in cabaret," she told me. "I was the assistant to an escape artist . . . Harry Blondini. I spent two and a half years being tied up. Harry loved ropes. He used to wear handcuffs in bed and he was the only guy I ever knew who took his showers hanging upside down in a straitjacket. He taught me everything he knew."

By now she was kneeling beside me, pulling the knots undone. "Why didn't you escape before?" I asked.

"There was no point. The door's barred from the outside. There's nothing I can do about that. And even if I could reach the window, it's too small for me to get through."

Too small for her, but when she gave me a leg up about fifteen minutes later, I found I could just squeeze through. Gott and Himmell hadn't bothered to lock it. Why should they? They'd left me tied up, and anyway, it didn't lead anywhere. It was five stories up and just too far below the roof for me to be able to scramble up there. I paused for a moment on the window ledge, my legs dangling inside, my head and shoulders in the cold evening air. I could see men working on a construction site in the distance and I shouted, trying to attract their attention. But they were too far away and, anyway, there was too much noise.

I looked down. It made my stomach heave a little. The pavement was a long, long way below. I could see the French windows that led back into the main living room about ten feet away. If I could break in through them, I could open the door and let Lauren out and at least we'd be on the way to safety. But the windows were too far away, and although they had a narrow ledge of their own, there was no way I could reach it. Unless . . .

This was a warehouse and like all the other warehouses it had a hook on a metal arm jutting out of the wall—in this case exactly halfway between the two windows and about a yard above them. In the old days it would have been used to hoist goods up from the street on a rope. The rope was gone, of course. But rope was at least one thing we had in plenty.

I squeezed myself back into the room.

"No way out—eh?" Lauren muttered.

"There might be." I explained what I had in mind.

"You're crazy," she said. "You can't do it."

"I've got to do it," I said. "Better crazy than dead."

Ten minutes later I was half in and half out again, but this time with a length of rope around my waist. We'd taken the rope that Himmell had used to tie us up and knotted it into a single length. There was a good twelve feet of it. I held the slack in my hand and now I began to swing it a bit like a lasso. Then I threw it, holding on to the end. The loop flew out toward the hook, missed, and fell. I pulled it in and tried again. I hooked it on the fourth attempt.

So there I am, five stories up, leaning out of a window. There's a rope leading from me to a hook and then back again, and I tie the end around my waist, too. Remember that isosceles triangle I mentioned? Well, it's a bit like that. The two windows are the lower corners. The hook is the point at the top. All I have to do is jump and the rope will swing me across like a pendulum from one side to the other. At least that's the general idea.

I didn't much like it. In fact I hated it. But I was running out of time and there didn't seem to be any other way.

I jumped.

For a giddy second I swung in the air, one shoulder scraping across the brickwork. But then my scrabbling hands somehow managed to grab hold of the edge of the French windows. I pulled, dangling in midair, supported only by the rope, my legs kicking at nothing. I pulled with all my strength. And then I was crouching on the ledge, trying hard not to look down, my heart beating in my chest like it would rather be someplace else.

I stayed where I was until I'd gotten my breath back, afraid of falling back into space. The ledge could only have been six inches wide and my whole body was pressed against the windowpanes. Without looking back into the street, I reached down and pulled off my shoe. Slowly I lifted it up. It was cold out there, but the sweat was running down inside my shirt. My eyes were fixed on the grand piano on the other side of the window. Somehow looking at it made me forget where I was and what I was doing. I held the shoe firmly in one hand, then brought it swinging forward. The heel hit the window, smashing it. I dropped the shoe into the room, then, avoiding the jagged edges of broken glass, slipped my hand through, found the lock, turned it. The window opened. With a sigh of relief I eased my way inside, then untied the rope and pulled it in after me.

I hadn't gotten very far, but at least I was still alive.

Gott and Himmell had left the tea things out. I put my shoe back on and took a swig of milk out of the jug. Then I went over to the door and drew back the bolt.

Lauren raised an eyebrow when she saw me. "So you made it?" she said.

"Yeah," I said. I would have said more, but for some reason my teeth were chattering at about one hundred and fifty miles per hour. It must have been even colder out there than I'd thought.

Lauren tried the door that led to the staircase. It was locked. Then she strolled across to the broken window and looked out.

"That's great, Nick," she drawled. "We're out of the closet but we can't get out of the room. There's nobody near enough to hear us shouting for help. You've sent our German friends on a wild-goose chase, and when they get back they're going to string you up and use you for target practice. We don't have enough rope to climb down with and we don't have any guns."

"That's about it," I agreed.

"Then you'd better think up something fast, kid." She pointed out of the window. "Because here they come right now."

THE LAST CHORD

I ran back over to the window. Lauren was right. The blue van was at the end of Bayly Street. It would have reached us already if a truck hadn't backed out of the construction site, blocking its path. Now it was stuck there while some guy in a yellow hat tried to direct the driver. Fortunately it was a tricky maneuver. They'd be stuck there for maybe another couple of minutes. How had they gotten back from Victoria so quickly? I played back what had happened in my mind and realized that my great escape had probably taken about an hour. It's amazing how time flies when you're having fun.

Lauren was in the kitchen, rummaging through the drawers. "What are you doing?" I asked.

"I'm looking for a knife." She held up a whisk.

"This is all I can find."

"They've got guns," I reminded her. "You're not going to get very far trying to whisk them."

"I know. I know." She threw the whisk over her shoulder. "So what are we going to do?"

What were we going to do? If we yelled for help, the only people who would hear us would be Gott and Himmell. The noise from the construction site would see to that. Even if we found a knife, it would be no defense against automatic pis-

tols. There was no way out and any minute now they'd be
coming in. I looked out of the window. The truck seemed to
be pinned at an angle across the road. The man in the yellow
hat was frantically giving directions, swatting at invisible flies.
I heard the truck grind into gear. It began to edge backward.
Soon the road would clear and the blue van would come. It
would come right underneath the window. I tried to remember where it had stopped when they brought me here. That
time they'd parked in front of the door. Would they park there
again? Perhaps.

"Lauren," I said.

"Yes?" She'd found a corkscrew and a dessert spoon.

"Quickly . . ."

The window that I'd broken in through was, like I said, a
French window. It came all the way down to the floor.
I looked out again. The truck had almost completed its
turn. The man in the yellow hat was walking away, his job
done.

"The piano," I said.

"The piano?"

"Come on!"

"Nick—this is no time for a concert."

"That's not what I have in mind."

I got my shoulder down to the piano and began to push. It
was on wheels which helped, but even so, it must have weighed
a ton. It was a Bechstein, a great chunk of black wood with
a gleaming white ivory smile. God knows how much it had

cost, but if this is what you needed to be a pianist, it made a good argument for taking up the triangle. Lauren had figured out what I was doing and now she stood there, staring.

"Honey," she said. "You can't be serious."

"Deadly serious," I said.

"Deadly," she agreed.

She came over and joined me. With the two of us pushing, the piano moved more easily. Inch by inch we drew closer to the open window. It was going to be a close fit, but the piano would just about slide through the frame. It occurred to me that that was probably how they'd gotten it in here in the first place. How long had it taken them to hoist it up? The return journey was certainly going to be a hell of a lot faster.

"Are you ready?" I asked.

"Yes."

I gazed over the top of the piano. The truck was in the clear now, rumbling quickly away. The blue van slid forward toward us. I flexed myself. There was a bust of Beethoven or someone on the piano. He was frowning as if he knew what was about to happen. The blue van drew closer, slowing down as it prepared to park.

We pushed with all our strength. The piano shot forward. Its back leg went over the ledge and with a hollow jangle it teetered on the brink, the pedals digging into the carpet. The van was almost level with us now. I pushed again. The piano resisted. Then, with a wave of relief, I felt it topple over backward. I can tell you now, Bechstein grand pianos are not built with any consideration for aerodynamics. It must have been a bizarre sight as it plummeted through the air: a huge black beast with three rigid legs and no wings. It flew for all of two seconds. Then it crashed fair and square into the van.

It was the Bechstein's last chord, but it was a memorable one. If you imagine someone blowing up an orchestra in the middle of Beethoven's Fifth, you'll get the general idea. It was an explosion of music—or a musical explosion. A *zing,* a *boom,* and a *twang* all rolled into one and amplified a hundred times. They heard it at the construction site. I doubt if there was anywhere in London that they didn't hear it.

The Bechstein was finished and I somehow doubted that the van would be doing much more traveling either. It hadn't been completely crushed, but it must have been disappointed. Steam was hissing out of the radiator and two of the tires were spinning away like giant coins. Black oil formed a sticky puddle around the wreckage. The exhaust pipe had shot away like a rocket and was lying about a hundred feet down the road. The whole twisted carcass of the van was covered in splinters of wood and wires. One of the piano's legs had shattered the front window. I didn't like to think what it had done to the driver.

"Quite a performance, honey," Lauren said.

"Concerto for piano and van," I muttered.

And now people did come running. Suddenly it was as if Bayly Street had become Piccadilly Circus. They came from the construction site, from the left, from the right, from just about everywhere. They looked at the carnage. Then they looked up. I leaned out of the window and waved.

It was about twenty minutes later that one of the construction workers appeared in the Germans' living room. He was carrying a pair of industrial pliers, which he must have used to cut through the two padlocks. Lauren and I were sitting on the sofa waiting for him.

"The piano . . ." He gaped at us. "Was it yours?"

"Sure," I said. "But don't worry. I wasn't much good at it anyway."

We walked out of the room, leaving him standing there. Well, what was he expecting? An encore?

We managed to slip away in the crowd, but not before I'd heard that—miraculously—nobody had been killed.

Apparently the driver of the van would have to be cut away from the steering wheel, while the passenger had managed to impale himself on the gearstick. A doctor had already arrived, but Gott and Himmell were more in need of a mechanic.

We got a taxi back to the office, where I picked up the real Maltesers and then we went straight on to Lauren's place. There were too many people looking for me in Fulham. From now on I'd have to keep my head down and my raincoat collar up. Lauren lived in a huge condominium in Baron's Court—about a ten-minute drive away. It was one of those great brick piles with fifty doorbells beside the front door and fifty people who don't know one another inside. She had a basement apartment that must have been all of five inches above the main Piccadilly subway line. Every time a train went past, the floor rumbled. Or maybe it was my stomach. I hadn't had a decent meal in twenty-four hours and I was hungry.

She left me in the living room while she went into the kitchen to fix supper. It was a cozy room in a theatrical sort of way, with a gas fire hissing in the grate, a kettle on the floor, and odd bits of clothes thrown just about everywhere. The furniture was old and tired, with a sofa that looked like it was waiting to swallow you up whole.

The walls were plastered with posters from theaters and music halls where Lauren had appeared, either as a singer or as an escape artist's assistant. It was a room with a past but no future. A room of rising damp and fading memories.

When she came back in she had changed into some sort of dressing gown and had brushed her hair back. For a woman old enough to be my grandmother she looked good. But then you should see my grandmother. The food she was carrying looked even better. She had it on a tray: omelettes, salad, cheese, fruit, a bottle of red wine for her, and Coke for me. We didn't say much while we ate. We were just glad to be there. Glad to be alive.

"Thanks," I said when I finished the omelette.

"I should thank you, Nick." Lauren poured herself some more wine. Her hand was trembling a little. "If it hadn't been for you . . . hell . . . they were going to kill me."

"You were the one who got out of the ropes," I reminded her. I glanced at the poster above the gas fire. It showed her with a flashy guy in a sequined straitjacket. He had greasy black hair, a mustache, and a toothpaste-advertisement smile. "Is that Harry Blondini?" I asked.

"Yes." She stood up and turned the stereo on. There was a click and a solo saxophone slithered through the room. She'd lit herself a cigarette and the smoke curled in time to the music. Her eyes told me everything I needed to know about the escape artist. But she told me anyway. "I loved him," she said. "For two years we worked together in the theater and we lived together for five. We were going to get married. But then, at the last minute, he ran off with a snake charmer. What did she have that I didn't—apart from two anacondas and a boa constrictor? That was the day before our wedding—the day before we were meant to tie the knot." She smiled a half smile. "Well, what should I have expected from an escape artist? He escaped. And he broke my heart.

"That was when I took up singing. I've been singing for twenty years, Nick. The same old songs. And in all that time I've only met two decent people. Johnny Naples and you. You're a nice kid, Nick. If I ever had a son, I'd have liked him to be like you.

"All I've ever wanted is a place of my own—maybe somewhere in the sun, like the South of France. Look at this place! Thirty feet underground—I never get to see the sun. And the Casablanca Club's the same. When they finally bury me, I'll actually be going up in the world. But it's a lousy world, Nick. Lousy . . ."

Maybe she'd had too much wine. I don't know. I'd asked her a simple question and she'd given me her life history. It was lucky I hadn't asked her anything tricky. We could have been there all night. I'd had enough. I was tired and I was dirty.

"I need a bath," I said.

She shook her head. "Of all the baths in all the towns in all the world, you have to walk into mine. There's no hot water."

"Then I'll just turn in."

"You can sleep on the sofa."

I took the tray back into the kitchen while she got me a couple of blankets. It was after she'd said good night and I was about to leave that I remembered the one question I'd meant to ask her. It was the whole reason I was there.

"Lauren," I said. "Back in the Casablanca Club . . . you were about to tell me something. You told me that you were out with Johnny when he saw something. It made the Maltesers and everything else make sense."

"That's right."

"Well . . . where were you?"

She paused, silhouetted in the doorway. "We were buying sausages," she said. "In Oxford Street. In Selfridges. In the food department."

SELFRIDGES

I don't like Oxford Street on the best of days—and let me tell you now, December 24, isn't one of them. Bond Street Station had been doing a good impersonation of the Black Hole of Calcutta and Lauren and I were glad to get out. But there was little relief outside. The Christmas rush had turned into the Christmas panic and the season seemed to have run pretty short of goodwill. Taxi drivers blasted their horns. Bus drivers leaned out of their windows and swore. You couldn't blame them. The traffic probably hadn't moved since December 22. There were so many people clawing their way along the pavement that you couldn't see the cracks. And everyone was carrying bulging bags. Of food, of decorations, of last-minute presents. I sighed. Herbert was still in jail.

He'd been there almost a week now. It looked like Christmas for me was going to be the Queen's speech and two frozen turkey croquettes.

But there was Selfridges with its white pillars, gold clocks, and flags fluttering across the roof. Somewhere inside the department store—in the food section—Johnny Naples had seen something that could have made him five million dollars. The thought cheered me up. I clutched the Maltesers. Lauren had loaned me a sort of shoulder bag and I had brought the candies with me. I wouldn't have felt easy without them.

We crossed the road, weaving between the traffic, and went in the front entrance. We were greeted by a cloud of sweet, sickly scent. This was the perfume department. They stocked all the perfumes in the world—and you could smell them all at once.

"Do you want to try this one?"

A pretty girl leaned over a counter, holding a bottle of aftershave toward me. I shook my head. She had a nice face. But she was a couple of years early.

It was hot inside Selfridges. The air had been chewed up by giant air-conditioners and spat out again. That was how it smelled. Secondhand. We went into the menswear department, following the signs that read FOOD.

"Come along and meet Santa Claus on the third floor in Santa's Workshop." The voice came out of invisible speakers, floating above the heat and the crowd.

"See all your favorite nursery rhymes. On the third floor. It's open now."

The food department was even worse than perfume and menswear. It was like nuclear war had just been announced. The shelves were being stripped, the salespeople bullied. I felt Lauren put her hand around my arm.

"This way," she said.

"I'm with you." But it was an effort. Relax for a minute

and I'd have been swept away on a river of rampant con-
sumerism, drowned in a lake of last-minute shopping.

"If we get separated, we can meet outside Marks and
Spencer," she said. "It's just across the road."

We made our way around the center section of the food
department, which was more or less like any supermarket.
There were separate bars here and there—juice, sandwiches,
and cookies—but most people were ignoring them. The meat
counter was at the back. There was a number in what looked
like a car headlight, hanging from the ceiling. Every few seconds there was a loud buzzing and the number changed. NOW
SERVING 1108, it read when we got there. It buzzed again:
1109. A clutch of housewives stared up at it. They were
all clutching tickets like they'd just gone in for some sort of
raffle.

So Selfridges sold sausages. I could see them through the
glass front of the cabinet. They looked very nice. I'm sure they
tasted great. But I didn't see what that had meant to Johnny
Naples. What did sausages have to do with the Falcon?

"Lauren . . ." I began.

"He was standing here," she said. "Then he suddenly
turned around and went that way." She pointed.

"You mean he went straight ahead?"

"No. We'd come from that way. He retraced his steps."

I followed in the footsteps of the dead dwarf. They took
me completely around the central supermarket, past the nuts,
and into the fruits, where some fancy items nestled among

the plums and Granny Smiths. BRAZILIAN LOQUATS, $3.50 LB., a sign read. That was probably a bargain if you knew what to do with a loquat. After that it was chocolates and then the checkout aisles. There was a row of six of them—with six women in brown coats and white straw hats. Five of them were ringing up prices on their registers like they were typing a novel. The sixth was just passing the purchases over a little glass panel in the counter and the prices were coming up automatically.

But I still hadn't seen anything that made me any the wiser. As far as I could see, Selfridges didn't even sell Maltesers.

"It was here," Lauren said.

"Here—what?" I sounded tired and depressed. Maybe that was because I was. It had been a wild-goose chase and I didn't even have enough money to go back to the meat counter and buy a wild goose.

"He knew," Lauren insisted. "He was standing where you were. And he suddenly smiled . . ."

I looked around and suddenly I wasn't smiling at all. There was a door opposite, leading into the street. Two men had just come in with the crowd. I think I saw them a few seconds before they saw me.

"Lauren," I whispered.

"What?"

I gestured. They'd changed since our first encounter, but I'd have recognized Gott and Himmell anywhere. They were still wearing identical suits—pale green with embroidered vests this time. But Himmell's left arm was now in a cast. Gott was walking with a cane. Both men had so many bandages on their face that I could hardly see any skin. But the skin I could see wasn't looking too healthy.

"You told them about the sausages," I said.

"Of course I told them," Lauren growled. "They were going to give me some more of their fairy cakes."

She'd told them. They'd come to look at the food department for themselves. And now they'd seen us.

"Let's move," I said.

We moved.

We ducked to the left—through an archway and down a flight of stairs past wines and spirits. Looking over my shoulder, I saw Gott giving Himmell some hurried instructions. A moment later I collided with a pair of little old ladies. With a little old screech they flew into a pile of crystallized fruit, which collapsed all around them. I didn't stop to apologize. "Manners maketh man," my father used to say. But Gott and Himmell weren't far behind. And they had every good reason to unmaketh me.

"Which way?" Lauren asked.

I stopped. There was a door leading out to Orchard Street, but it was blocked with about a dozen people fighting their way in. That left us a choice of three or four directions.

"Wait a minute, Lauren . . ." I said.

I was about to say that this was ridiculous. Gott and Himmell might be crazy, but there was no way they were going to try anything. Not in the middle of Selfridges on Christmas Eve. I was going to say that they'd wait for us outside and that we'd have to give them the slip when we left. I was going to say—

But right then a cabinet of watches behind my head exploded. Just like that. Glass flew out in glittering fragments. A salesgirl screamed. I spun around. Gott was standing at the top of the stairs. He was holding a gun. It was silenced, so there had been no bang. But it was smoking. And nobody had noticed. They hadn't heard anything and they were too busy with their shopping to stop anyway.

"That way!" I cried.

Lauren went one way. I went another.

She must have missed the way I was pointing. She ran down a corridor back into menswear while I made for the escalator. There was no time to hesitate. And perhaps it was for the best. We had a better chance of getting away if we split up.

"The meeting place for customers who have lost their companions is on the lower ground floor . . ." The voice poured soothingly out of the speakers. Lauren had certainly lost me. But unless I lost the Germans, our only meeting place would be the morgue.

The escalator was slow. Impossibly slow. And I couldn't run up it as I was hemmed in by shoppers on both sides. I squatted down and looked back, wondering if Gott and Himmell had missed me. They hadn't. There was no sign of Gott, but Himmell was standing there, taking aim. This time I think I heard the *phutt* as the bullet came out. Just above my head, a white box with the figure "1" on it suddenly shattered and the light went out inside. I reached the top of the escalator and swung around past a collection of hats, then onto a second escalator with a third after that. On the third floor, not even knowing if Himmell was still behind me, I ran forward—through the children's clothes department.

I stopped to catch my breath at another of the archways. There were fewer people up here. After all, who buys children clothes for Christmas except relatives who should know better? I couldn't see Himmell and I thought I'd lost him, but then a plastic dummy about three inches away from me suddenly lurched over backward with a hole in its forehead and fell with a clatter of broken plastic. Gott had gone after Lauren. But Himmell was still after me. I turned and ran.

And now there were more people. I didn't mind that. The more the merrier, as far as I was concerned. It took me a few seconds to realize where I was heading and by then it was too late to go anywhere else. There was a sign:

To Santa's Workshop

Now I remembered the loudspeaker announcement. Santa Claus and my favorite nursery rhymes. I'd almost prefer to spend the afternoon with Himmell.

The straggle of people had become a line. I ignored them. A few people protested as I ran past them, but most had little children with them and they weren't going to start a fight. I ran on, past a red screen and down a brightly lit corridor. It led into a day-care area where a woman was standing behind a desk, gently controlling the crowd. She called out to me, but I ignored her, sliding down a ramp to crash into a brick wall. Fortunately, the brick wall was made out of cardboard. I glanced back, hoping that I'd at last shaken Himmell. But there he was, one arm in a white cast jutting out of his body as if he'd been caught in the middle of a karate chop. His other arm was jammed into his pocket. I knew what it was holding.

I dived into Santa's workshop. I didn't like it. But I had no choice.

It was packed inside, with everyone talking in low voices while nursery rhymes played on the loudspeaker system. There were a lot of models—Elizabethan villages and that sort of thing, illustrating the rhymes. They'd fixed them up with those little dolls that do jerky movements. They didn't fool me. Jack and Jill looked slightly ill, while Miss Muffet seemed to be having convulsions. The models were arranged so that the passage swerved around with dark sections and light sections. I moved as quickly as I could, pushing aside anyone who got in the way. Nobody complained. With their arms full of little kids asking inane questions, they had more than enough to worry about.

So had I. I was trapped in Santa's workshop and I needed an exit. I saw one, but it was blocked by a security guard. I turned another corner past Little Jack Horner and stopped again next to Humpty-Dumpty. There was no sign of Himmell. Perhaps he was waiting for me outside. Some of the children were more interested in me than in the models. I suppose I must have looked pretty strange, panting and sweating—the way you do when you're running for your life. I took a couple of steps farther into the workshop. At the same moment, Humpty-Dumpty exploded in all directions, his arms and legs soaring into the air. All the king's soldiers and all the king's men certainly won't be able to put that one together again, I thought as I forced my way through the crowd.

And still nobody knew anything was wrong. It was incredible. But it was also gloomy. And if you've got your eyes on a ship with thirty or so white mice on it, maybe you won't notice when a private detective's younger brother is being murdered behind you. I looked around. Himmell had been held up by a tough-looking gang of seven-year-olds. Still walking backward, my eyes fixed on him, I turned a corner. Somebody seized me. I was jerked off my feet. I twisted around again. I couldn't believe it. I'd bumped into Santa Claus and he'd pulled me onto his lap.

Now he looked at me with cheerful eyes and a white-bearded smile. He really was the complete department-store Santa: red hat, red suit, bulging stomach, and bad breath.

"You're a bit big for Santa, aren't you?" he asked in a jolly Santa voice.

"Let me go," I said, squirming on his lap.

But he held on to me. I got the feeling he was enjoying himself. "And what do you want for Christmas?" he asked.

"I want to get away from a guy who wants to kill me."

He laughed at that. There were a whole lot of people in Santa's chamber, and if I hadn't been so angry I'd have been red with embarrassment. A little girl—she couldn't have been more than six—pointed at me and laughed. Her parents took a photograph.

"Ho-ho—" Santa boomed out.

He didn't make the third "ho."

There was another quiet *phutt* and he keeled over. I threw myself onto the floor. Himmell was on the other side of the chamber, reloading his gun. Nobody was looking at him. They were looking at Santa, at the body twitching on the chair, at the red stuff that was staining his beard. The little girl began to cry.

"Don't worry," I said. "Santa's okay."

Santa died. I fled.

I got out of the workshop just as the people began to scream in earnest. I could still hear them as I ran across a floor of women's clothes, searching for a way out.

"Security to third floor, please. Security to third floor." The calm, unruffled voice came over the loudspeakers as I spotted a fire exit, pulled it open, and found myself in a quiet

stairwell. I wanted to go back down to the street level, but even as I stood there, I could hear the tramp of feet coming up. They didn't sound like shoppers. They were too fast, too determined. It had to be the security guards. I looked up. The stairway was clear. I made for the fourth floor.

Through a door, along a corridor, through another door, and suddenly I'd burst into the toy department. I was tired now. I couldn't run much more. And the noise and the color of the toys somehow drained away the last of my strength. Robots buzzed and clicked. Electric organs played hideous tunes. Computer games bleeped and whined. Something whipped past my head. I thought it was another bullet and jerked back, sending a whole pile of robots flying. But it was only a sales clerk with a paper glider. The robots writhed on the floor. I shrugged and staggered off into the toys.

I was sure I'd lost Himmell now. From toys I went into sports—first the clothes, then billiard tables, weights, golf clubs, and hockey sticks. I rested against a counter that had been set up for a special promotion. There was a sign reading:

DISCOVER THE DELIGHTS OF

DEEP-SEA DIVING

A young salesman was showing an American couple the latest equipment: masks, wet suits, harpoons.

"The harpoon works on compressed air," I heard him say. "You just pull the lever here, load it like this, and then—"

And then Himmell appeared. He'd come from nowhere. He was only about ten feet away from me. I had nowhere else to run. He had his hand in his pocket and now he brought it up, the jacket coming with it. He smiled. He was going to shoot me through the pocket. Then he would just walk away. And no one would know.

I lunged to one side, grabbed the harpoon gun, then wheeled around. The salesman shouted. I pressed the trigger.

The gun shuddered in my hands. The harpoon shot out, snaking a silver rope behind it. For a moment I thought I'd missed. The harpoon seemed to sail over Himmell's shoulder. But then I saw that one prong had gone through his suit, pinning him to the wall. The American stared at me.

"Good gun!" I said. And dropped it. Himmell lunged forward, but he wasn't going anywhere. He was stuck there like a German calendar.

"You little . . . !" he began.

I didn't want to hear him. I found another fire exit and this time I managed to get out of Selfridges without being stopped. I crossed the road and made my way around the front of Marks and Spencer. I was relieved to find Lauren waiting for me.

"What kept you?" she said.

"You got away okay?" I asked.

"Sure. Gott could hardly walk, let alone run. Himmell was in better shape."

"Yeah," I agreed. "He was."

Lauren sighed. "Well, that was a waste of time," she said. "We didn't learn anything."

I thought back to the food department, to the things I had seen. And suddenly I understood. It was as if I'd known all along, only someone had to sock me on the jaw to make me realize it. I smiled. Johnny Naples must have smiled that way. Lauren saw it. "Come on . . ." I said.

The same taxis and the same buses were jammed in the same place as we crossed Oxford Street again. We got back on the subway. It would take us to South Kensington, where we'd get a bus.

I knew. But I had to be sure.

INFORMATION

"The bar code," I said.

"The what?"

"Those little black-and-white lines you get on the things you buy."

"What about them?"

I pulled the Maltesers out of the shoulder bag and showed them to Lauren. "Look," I said. "You see? It's got a bar code."

"So what?"

"That's what they were using in Selfridges. The girl was passing her products over a scanner and the scanner was telling the cash register how much the products cost." Lauren looked blank, so I went on. "Maybe if you pass *this* bar code over a scanner, it'll do something different."

"Like what?"

"I don't know. That's what we're going to find out."

I needed a science lesson in a hurry and for once in my life I was sorry school had shut for the holidays. But I had another idea. Journalists write about technology and things like that. They know a little bit about everything. And I knew a journalist: Clifford Taylor, the guy who'd interviewed

Herbert and me. He'd been at the Falcon's funeral, too, so I figured he must still work on the same newspaper, the *Fulham Express*. That was where we were heading now. I had to be sure that I was right.

Nobody reads the *Fulham Express,* but everybody who lives in Fulham gets it. They don't have any choice. It's one of those free newspapers that come uninvited along with a shower of plumbers' business cards, taxi telephone numbers, and special offers from *Reader's Digest.* It's delivered every Wednesday in the morning. And you can see it every Wednesday, in the afternoon, stuffed into trash cans or drinking up the dirt in the gutter.

We took a bus all the way down the Fulham Road, past Herbert's flat, to the bottom—Fulham Broadway. This was the Fulham Road at its worst: dirty in the rain, dusty in the sun, always run-down and depressing. I'd occasionally walked past the office of the *Fulham Express,* but I'd never been inside before. It was on the main road, next to a bank. Lauren and I climbed up a flight of stairs and found ourselves in a single, rectangular room with a printing press at one end and a photocopying machine at the other. In the middle there were two tables, piled high with newspaper clippings. The room must have been a dance studio at one time because it had mirrors all the way down one wall, making it seem twice as big as it was. Even so, it was small.

Clifford was there, feverishly working on a story that in a few days someone would use to wrap their fish and chips. I coughed, and when he didn't respond, I walked up to him. He was the only person there.

"Clifford . . ." I said.

"Yes?" He looked up.

"You don't remember me?"

"If you're from the dance class, you're too early. The newspaper has the room until five—"

"I'm Nick Diamond."

He took his glasses off and wiped them. There were sweat stains under his arms and his acne had grown worse. He was a mess. I doubted if he could even spell "personal hygiene."

"Nick who?" he asked.

"Diamond." I glanced at Lauren, who shrugged. "You interviewed me," I reminded him. "My brother's a private detective."

Now he did remember. "Of course! Absolutely! How's it going? There's not much call for private detectives in Fulham—"

"I know," I interrupted. Clifford liked talking. When he interviewed us, he'd talked more than we had. "I was wondering if you could help me," I said.

"Sure. Sure."

"It's a sort of scientific question. Do you know anything about shopping?"

"Shopping?" He frowned. "I don't think I know anyone called Shopping. There's Chopin . . . but he was a composer, not a scientist."

"No." I sighed. "I'm talking about shops. And about bar codes. I want to know how they work."

Clifford ran a hand through his hair. There wasn't that much left for him to run it through. In fact, he had more dandruff than actual hair. "Okay." He leaned back and put his feet up on the desk. "Technology is mainly about one thing: information. The electronic storage and transmission of information. Computers store information. Satellites send information. But all this information isn't written out like a book. No way. It's turned into what's known as digital information.

"What does digital information look like? Well, in the old days it would have been a hole punched into a computer tape. There are holes in the modern compact disc, too—although they're too small to see. And a bar code is another form of digital information. It's as simple as that.

"All products have a bar code on them these days. If you look at them, you'll see that there's a number with thirteen digits underneath it. That's all a bar code is. A number—a unique number that can tell the computer everything it needs to know."

I'd taken out the box of Maltesers again while he talked. Clifford's eyes lit up when he saw it. He leaned forward and took it.

"Take this box," he said. "Here's the bar code on the bottom." He pointed to the strip of blue-and-white lines in the left-hand corner. "Part of it would tell the computer that this is a product made by Mars. Another part of it would tell the computer that it's a box of Maltesers, that it weighs so much and costs so much. It could even remind the shopkeeper to stock up."

"How does the computer read the bar code?" I asked.

"Well, that's all done with lasers," Clifford explained. "There's a sort of little window built into the counter near the cash register. The person who's sitting there passes the box of Maltesers—or whatever—over it. Now, behind the window there's a laser scanner. The salesclerk could use a light-emitting diode, which is the same sort of thing, but either way, the light hits the bar code. Are you with me so far?"

I wasn't sure, but I nodded anyway. If I'd learned one thing from science lessons at school, it was this. When scientific types start explaining things, it's hard enough to follow. But when they start explaining the explanations, that's when you really get lost.

"All right." He nodded. "The light beams hit the bar code. Now, the dark lines don't reflect light. Only the white ones do that. So only some of the light gets reflected. And somewhere inside that little window there's a photodetector, which is a clever machine that produces a pulse of electricity whenever you shine a light on it. Do you see? As you slide the bar code over the window, the shining light hits the lines. Some of it is reflected back onto the photodetector, which gives out a 'bleep' for every white line. It's the 'bleep' that's the digital information sent to the computer. Almost like Morse code. And that's how the computer knows what the product is!"

He stopped triumphantly and sneezed. Lauren reached out for the Maltesers and he gave them to her. She turned them over and examined the bar code.

"Could you use the bar code like a . . . a key?" I asked. That was the word the Fat Man had used. He had said he was looking for a key.

"Absolutely!" the journalist said. "That's just what it is, really."

"But could it open something—like a safe?"

"It depends how you programmed your computer. But the answer's yes. It could open a safe. Play Space Invaders. Make the tea. And so on."

They open the . . . I'd asked the Professor what the Maltesers did, and that was what he'd said before he caught himself. It was all clicking together. A key. A code known only to the Falcon. A safe. Johnny Naples had guessed the day he went to Selfridges. Now I remembered the words he'd written down on the scraps of paper I'd found in his room. *Digital . . . photodetector . . . light-emitting diode.* Clifford Taylor had used them all in his explanation.

I'd always thought that it was the Maltesers themselves that were the answer to the riddle. But I'd been wrong and I should have guessed. When Johnny Naples had bought the envelope at Hammetts, he'd done something else. He'd bought a pair of scissors. Why? To cut out the bar code. That was all he needed. He just had to feed it into . . .

But that was one thing I still didn't know.

"I do hope I've been helpful," the journalist said.

"Sure," I said. "More helpful than you'd guess."

"Is there a story in it?"

I nodded. "An international master criminal, a gang of crooks, a fortune in diamonds? There's a story all right."

Clifford Taylor sighed. "I'm afraid I can't use it. It's much too exciting for the *Fulham Express*. But look out for the next edition. I'm doing a very interesting piece on the effectiveness of one-way traffic systems in Chelsea."

"I can hardly wait," I said.

We left him at his desk and went back down the stairs. It was only when we got to the bottom that Lauren's hand flew to her mouth. "I've left the Maltesers upstairs!" she exclaimed. "Hang on, honey . . ."

I watched her run up the stairs and into the newspaper office. About a minute later, she reappeared, waving the Maltesers. "I must be out of my mind!" she said. "How could I leave them?"

I thought no more of it. That was definitely a mistake.

We were near Herbert's flat, so I decided to go in and get some fresh clothes. It was easier for Lauren to take the subway straight to Baron's Court, so we parted company outside

Fulham Broadway Station. It was a beautiful day. Cold but with a brilliant sun. Lauren stopped outside the station almost like she was afraid to go in.

"Nick . . ." she said.

"Yes?"

"What I said that night—I want you to know that I meant it. You're a nice boy. You deserve the best."

I stared at her, then laughed uneasily. "What is this?" I said. "I'll only be an hour or so. You're talking like I'm never going to see you again."

"Sure." She shook her head. "Forget it."

She went into the station.

I walked all the way up the Fulham Road, past the cemetery, and on to the flat. As I walked, I thought. I understood so much now. What the Maltesers meant and why everybody wanted them. The only trouble was, if the Maltesers really were a sort of digital key, how was I to find the digital door? And there was something else that puzzled me. Who had shot Johnny Naples in the first place? My money was on the Fat Man. If it had been Gott and Himmell, they'd have told me when I was their prisoner. After all, they'd told me about Lawrence without blinking an eye. But at the same time, I couldn't believe it. I just couldn't see the Fat Man getting his hands dirty that way. It wasn't his style. So if not him—who?

I checked the bag. At least the Maltesers were safe. Right now that was all that mattered.

It was around three when I reached the flat. I slipped in

as quickly as I could. The fewer people who saw me go in, the better. I didn't mean to stay there long—just long enough to pull on a fresh shirt and a new pair of socks and make a clean getaway. I went up the stairs. The office door was open. I went in.

There were four thugs in there waiting for me. One was behind the door. He kicked it shut after I'd gone through it, so when I turned around there was no way out. I'd have given my right arm for a way out. If I hung around there much longer they'd probably tear it off anyway. The four thugs were all wearing extra-large suits. That was because they were extra-large thugs. I was once taught at school that Man evolved from the ape and all I can say is that these four had a long way to catch up. They were big, heavy, and brutal, with unintelligent eyes and thick lips. They were all chewing gum, their lower jaws sliding up and down in unison. "Are you Nick Diamond?" one of them asked.

"Me?" I said. "No . . . no! I'm not Nick Diamond. I'm . . . er . . . the delivery boy."

"What are you delivering?" a second demanded.

"Um . . ." I was having to think on my feet. Any minute now I'd be thinking on my back. If I was still conscious. "I'm a singing telegram!" I exclaimed, brilliantly. "Happy birthday to you, happy birth . . ." I tried to sing, but the words died in my throat. The four thugs weren't convinced. "Come on, guys," I pleaded. "Gimme a break."

"Yeah—your legs," the third one said.

They all laughed at that. I'd heard more cheerful sounds on a ghost train. They were still laughing as they closed in on me.

"You're making a big mistake," I said.

The man behind the door was the first to reach me. He grabbed my shoulder with one hand and lifted me clean off my feet. "There's no mistake, sunshine," he said. "The Fat Man wants to see you."

IN THE FOG

I discovered that the four thugs were called Lenny, Benny, Kenny, and Fred. Lenny was in charge. He was the one with the driver's license. He'd parked the car outside the flat. It was a Volkswagen Bug. After we'd all piled in it I was surprised it was able to move. I certainly wasn't. I was on the backseat between Benny and Kenny. Things were so tight that if they'd both breathed in at the same time, I'd have been crushed. The Maltesers were still in my shoulder bag, but now the shoulder bag was on Fred's lap. Lenny was driving. I was being "taken for a ride," as they say. And I had a nasty feeling I'd only been given a one-way ticket.

We drove out of town, west toward Richmond. Lenny had made a telephone call before we left, so I knew the Fat Man would be waiting for me. It looked like he was going to have a long wait. These heavies really were heavy and the car could only manage thirty miles an hour on the level. Not that I was in any hurry. In fact, my only hope was that the engine would finally explode under the pressure. I could hardly see them "taking me for a ride" on a bus.

"You can't do this to me," I protested. "I'm underage. I'm only a kid. I've got my whole life ahead of me."

"That's what you think." Lenny sneered.

"But I've got money," I said. "I could make you guys rich."

"Sure." Lenny swung the steering wheel. "You can leave it to us in your will."

The car turned off the main road and began to follow a winding lane through what looked like the remains of an industrial complex. It was still pretty complex, but I figured it hadn't been industrial for a hundred years. It was a network of Victorian buildings, most of them burned out. Another bit of London that was falling down.

The lane led down to the river. Suddenly we came to the end of the blacktop and I could hear gravel crunching underneath the tires. The car bounced up and down. The four thugs bounced in their seats. The springs screamed for mercy. We drove right up to the edge of the river. Then Lenny put on the handbrake. We'd arrived.

"Out," he ordered.

He'd produced a gun from somewhere and I don't need to tell you what it was pointing at. If you've ever looked into the single eye of a gun barrel, you'll know it's no fun. The devil must have an eye like that.

"Walk," Lenny said.

I walked. We'd stopped in a space about the size of a parking lot, only the bug was the only car parked there. It was another building site—more luxury houses for the Thames. But they'd only gotten as far as the foundations and a few pieces of the framework. The iron girders hemmed us in like we were on the stage of a Greek amphitheater, only there was no audience. The light was fading, and to complete the picture—or maybe to obliterate it—the fog had rolled in across the water. It carried the smell of salt and dead fish in its skeleton fingers, and when it touched my neck I shivered. I couldn't see across to the other side of the Thames. Which meant that anyone on the other side couldn't see me. I was alone with just about the four nastiest customers you could ever hope not to meet.

There was a low hiss as one of them lit a paraffin lamp. It threw a circle of hard, white light. They'd set it all up in advance. I didn't understand it—but somehow I didn't like it much. There was a wooden chair about twelve feet away from the edge of the river and an old iron bathtub right in front of it. The bathtub was quite deep. It came to about the same level as the chair. Nearby, there was a pile of brown paper sacks. Kenny picked one up and tore it open. Gray powder flooded out. At the same time, Benny walked forward carrying a hose. Water was already spluttering out, liquid mercury in the strange, harsh light. Cement, water, a bathtub, a chair, and the River Thames. Now I understood it all—and I liked it even less.

"Sit down," Lenny said.

He waved the gun toward the chair. I walked forward, the soles of my shoes squelching on the wet gravel. The four men never stopped watching me. They weren't getting any pleasure out of this. They were just doing a job. Mind you, I wasn't getting any pleasure out of it either—and I wasn't being paid. But there was nothing I could do. I sat down on the chair. It was so close to the bathtub that my legs had to go in it. Out of the corner of my eye I could see Kenny and Benny mixing the cement. If I ever get out of this one, I thought to myself, I'll take the first flight to Australia. My parents might not have been ideal company, but they'd never tried to kill me. At least, not so you'd notice.

"Look, Lenny—" I began, trying to be reasonable.

"Button it, kid," he snapped.

Kenny and Benny came over, each carrying a large bucket of wet cement. They glanced at Lenny. He nodded. As one, they tipped them over. The stuff poured out sluggishly, like cold oatmeal. It splattered down into the bath, covering my shoes and rising about five inches up my legs. I could feel it seeping through my socks. It was icy. And it was heavy, too. My shoes were pressing against my toes. They were only sneakers and already the cement was oozing through them. I wiggled my toes. Lenny pressed the gun against the side of my neck. "Keep still," he said.

"But it's wet . . ." I complained.

"Don't worry, kid. It's quick-drying. You keep still and it'll set in no time."

Two more buckets followed the first and two more went after them. By the time Kenny and Benny had finished, the cement came all the way up to my knees. If anyone had seen me—sitting there with my legs in a bath staring out across the Thames—they'd have thought I was crazy. But nobody would see me. It was dark now. And the fog had grown thicker. Like the cement.

Lenny wasn't even bothering to massage my neck with his gun anymore. The cement had almost set. I experimented. Carefully I tried to lift my right foot. I couldn't do it. That was when I began to get really afraid. Talk about having one foot in the grave—I had both feet and most of my legs. I was glued to the bathtub and I knew that any minute now they'd pick it up and drop it into the river. I—it—we would sink like a stone. I'd spend the rest of eternity in an upright position.

They say that when a man drowns, his whole life flashes before him. Mine did that now, but it was all over in about five seconds. That made me sad. It had been a short life and I'd spent far too much of it at school.

I heard a sort of glugging sound coming from the Thames. That made my ears prick up. A boat. It was getting closer. For a moment I was hopeful. It might be a river-police boat. Or perhaps a dredger of some sort. But Fred had been waiting for it. The gray curtains of fog were pushed aside by the bow of a sleek white cruiser. A rope was thrown out of the darkness. A gangplank was slid over the edge and made steady on the bank. The Fat Man walked down it.

He was dressed in a dinner jacket with a mauve bow tie and a white silk scarf hanging loose around his neck. He nodded at Fred and the others and then strolled over to me. Without saying a word, he leaned down and tapped the concrete with his knuckles. That made my heart lurch. The stuff was already solid. I couldn't even feel my feet. He straightened up. The four thugs formed a rough circle around us. And I can tell you now, circles just don't come any rougher.

"No wisecracks today, Nicholas?" the Fat Man demanded. "Nothing funny to say?"

"You're a loony, Fat Man," I said.

"And you, my boy, are a fool. You were lucky to escape alive from the Hotel Splendide. But now your time has run out."

"What have you got against me?" I asked. "What did I ever do to you?"

"You lied to me," the Fat Man said. "Worse still, you defied me. I gave you forty-eight hours to find something for me. Find it you did not."

"Well . . ." I said. "How about a second chance?"

He sniffed. At the same time, Fred moved forward. He'd opened the shoulder bag and taken out the Maltesers. He handed them to the Fat Man. The Fat Man looked at the bottom, holding them to the light so that he could read something. "Perfect!" he whispered. That threw me. How had he found out about the Maltesers? He'd never mentioned them before. He must have read the expression on my face because he smiled. "You're wondering how I discovered what was inside the dwarf's package?" he asked. He turned around to the boat. "Professor!"

I peered through the swirling fog. A second figure appeared at the top of the gangplank and made his way unsteadily down. He stood at the edge of the circle of light, blinking at me. Quentin Quisling, the Professor. He shook his head. "You gave me the wrong box, sir," he said in an accusing tone of voice.

"So the Professor came to me," the Fat Man continued. "A wise decision. A very wise decision. Did you know that the Professor designed them in the first place? You see, the Falcon needed a key—but a key that didn't look like a key. He had too many enemies. The Professor created the bar code—"

"But why Maltesers?" I asked. The information wasn't going to be much use to me, but I wanted to know.

The Professor shrugged. "I like Maltesers," he said.

"And now I have them." The Fat Man smiled. The smile stretched his skin across his cheekbones like an elastic band. "And soon, very soon, the Professor will tell me what they open—"

"And then you'll kill him, too," I interrupted. I had nothing to lose. I was only minutes away from the end. I could feel the chill of the cement spreading through my entire body. I turned to the Professor. "You don't think the Fat Man will share the money with you, do you?" I said. "Once you tell him your secret, you'll be joining the line at the bottom of the Thames."

"We'll split the money fifty-fifty . . ." the Professor mumbled, but I could see he had his doubts.

"I'll see you in hell, Professor," I said.

The Fat Man was furious. His face had gone white and the veins in his neck were standing out so far they were threatening to snap his bow tie. "Throw him in!" he yelled.

He stepped back. At once, Lenny, Benny, and Kenny moved in on me. They bent down and a moment later I was in the air, bath and all, being carried toward the Thames. Don't let me kid you. I like to think I'm smart. Sometimes I act older than I am. But right then I would have screamed and cried and torn my hair out if I'd thought for a single second that screaming and crying and tearing my hair out would do any good.

The river drew closer. The Fat Man watched. The three men shuffled forward.

They were about six feet from the edge of the water when a spotlight cut through the fog and the darkness. It came from high up, somewhere behind me. It was hard to tell. The night seemed to rip apart, torn into shreds by the beam. The fog boiled furiously in its grip. The gangsters stopped as if frozen.

There was a crackle in the air. Then a voice boomed out, amplified by a bullhorn.

"This is the police. Stay where you are. You're surrounded."

Lenny, Benny, and Kenny dropped me. I crashed to the ground but remained standing up. The Fat Man ran for the boat. He still had the Maltesers. The Professor stumbled after him. Lenny took out his gun and fired in the direction of the spotlight. I tried to dive for cover, but I was about as capable of that as an oak tree. There was an answering shot. Lenny was blown off his feet. His gun clattered to the ground.

"Don't move," the voice commanded. *"We're armed."* It was a bit late to be telling Lenny that.

The Fat Man had reached the boat and turned around, stretching out a hand for the Professor. But the Professor was nowhere near him. Half drunk and nearsighted, he ran forward, missed the gangplank, and dived into the Thames. Benny, Kenny, and Fred scattered and ran for cover. But now the whole area was swarming with men. They were throwing black shadows as they sprinted through the glare.

The Professor couldn't swim. He was floundering in the water, shouting for help. But the Fat Man couldn't wait. The police had almost reached the boat.

The boat's engine roared and it swung away from the bank. At the same moment the Professor let out a ghastly scream. He'd been in the water. He'd been close to the propellers. Too close. I was glad I couldn't see what the Fat Man had accidentally done to him.

Benny, Kenny, and Fred were arrested. I saw them thrown to the ground. The whole construction site was lit up. And I was still standing in the middle of it all, knee-deep in cement.

And then I felt the bathtub being dragged slowly toward

the river. I couldn't believe it. There was a figure squatting, struggling, pulling the bathtub along the gravel. With me in it.

But then I heard a familiar voice. Snape's voice.

"No, Boyle," he said. "You can't push him in. We've come here to rescue him. Go to the car and get a chisel."

IN THE BATH

Snape and Boyle drove me back to the apartment. I was cold. I was wet. And I was fed up. My pants, sneakers, and socks were ruined and my legs weren't feeling much better. My throat was sore and my nose was blocked. They'd gotten my feet out of the cement, but I could still feel the cement in my blood and there was nothing they could do about that. And I'd lost the Maltesers. It had been a bad day. I was glad it was over. If I'd known it was going to be a day like that, I'd have stayed in bed.

They came in with me and I made them some coffee. While the kettle was boiling I tried to call Lauren. I thought she might be worried about me. But there was no answer. I flicked on the hot-water tank for a bath and went back downstairs. Snape and Boyle had made themselves comfortable in the office. I fixed us three cups of coffee and took them in. I didn't like them and they didn't like me. But like it or not, they'd saved my life. The least I could do was give them a cup of coffee.

"All right," I said. "How did you find me?"

"We were watching the flat," Snape told me. "We saw you go in and we saw you taken out. Lucky for you. We followed you to the Thames. When we saw what was going on, Boyle here called for backup on the radio."

"Why were you watching the flat?" I asked.

Snape let out a sniff of laughter. "Why do you think? In the last few days we've been receiving some of the craziest reports I've heard in thirty years. A young boy blows up a hotel in the Portobello Road. A young boy pushes a grand piano out of a fifth-floor window. A young boy goes berserk in Selfridges and leaves forty hysterical children and a dead Santa Claus behind him. You'd think London was crawling with lethal young boys. Except they all fit the same description. Yours."

"I can explain," I said.

"I'm delighted to hear it. You've been making life very difficult for me. You've upset Boyle—"

"I'm upset," Boyle agreed.

"—and you've done more damage than the Germans managed in two world wars. And I thought your brother was a menace!"

"Where is Herbert?" I asked.

Snape's eyes narrowed at that. "We released him at lunchtime. We couldn't hold him. To be honest, we didn't want to."

"Well, I haven't seen him."

I wasn't particularly bothered just then. It was strange that Herbert should have just disappeared, but I could understand it. He'd probably gone to Auntie Maureen in Slough. He'd hide out there until the heat was off. I shivered. Herbert hadn't paid the gas bill for the flat. The heat had been off for two weeks.

"Did he tell you everything?" I asked.

"Well, let's just say that Herbert and canaries have a lot in common."

Snape held out a hand. "I want the Maltesers," he said.

"I don't have them," I said. "The Fat Man took them." Snape's eyes narrowed a little more. "If you don't believe me, you can search my bag."

"I already have," Boyle muttered.

"The Fat Man took them," I repeated. "When you arrest him you can get them from him."

"Arrest him?" Snape twisted his neck until the bone clicked. "That may not be so easy."

"Why not?"

"It's a question of evidence, lad. We haven't got anything on him. Nothing concrete—"

"What about the stuff he was burying me in?"

"You don't understand!" Snape was distressed. "He'll deny he was ever there. He'll say it was a case of mistaken identity . . . in the fog. He'll have an alibi."

I shook my head in disbelief. "So that's it, then," I said. "If the Fat Man goes free, he'll find the diamonds and that'll be the end of it."

"You should have given us the Maltesers in the first place," Boyle said.

"Sure." I nodded. "And if the Fat Man had come strolling

in and claimed them as lost property, I suppose you'd have handed them over."

That made Boyle scowl again. But Snape stood up. "You've got a lot of questions to answer," he said.

"Are you arresting me?"

"No. You've had enough for one day. We'll talk to you next week. Like you say, the Fat Man has the Maltesers and that's the end of it. We'll be in touch."

I showed them to the door. Snape stopped in the doorway and turned around. "Merry Christmas," he said.

I'd forgotten until then. It was Christmas Eve. "Yeah . . . Merry Christmas, Chief Inspector," I said. "And to you, Boyle."

Boyle grunted. He probably didn't even know what Christmas was.

An hour later I was lying in hot water with soap bubbles up to my neck and Herbert's plastic duck floating around my feet. My body wasn't a pretty sight just then. What with the ropes, the cement, and the general manhandling, I had more bruises than I cared to count. But it felt good in the bath. I needed to relax. It was time for some serious thinking.

What did the Maltesers unlock?

I knew the answer. I knew I knew the answer.

It had to be something near Herbert's apartment. Johnny Naples had left Notting Hill Gate with the Maltesers and a pair of scissors. By then he'd found the answer. He knew where he was going and he went to Fulham. But he'd been followed—and rather than lead anyone to his destination, he'd come to us. So it had to be something near. But what was there near the apartment connected with the Falcon?

Four days later we'd found Naples dying. He'd managed to say two things: "The Falcon" and "the sun." I assumed it was sun—with a *u*. Henry von Falkenberg didn't have a son . . . at least, not one that we'd heard about. But what did the sun have to do with the Falcon? Nothing . . . unless he'd been talking about another falcon. Maybe not a man. A bird. Or a statue of a bird.

And then I thought about the Maltesers themselves and about a phrase that Clifford Taylor had used. The journalist had described the laser as "the shining light." The sun was a shining light, too. But the phrase bothered me. I'd seen those words somewhere before. The Maltesers.

When the Fat Man had taken them, he'd looked on the bottom. I'd already tricked the Professor once. He'd told the Fat Man to find something, to check that they were the real ones. Henry von Falkenberg would have had to mark them in some way. And there was an easy way.

You'll see that there's a number with thirteen digits underneath.

That was what the journalist had said. And I knew that

number. I'd read it so many times that I'd learned it by heart: 3521 201 000000. That number was the final clue.

I pulled the bath plug out with my toes and wrapped a towel around my body. Then, still dripping water, I went downstairs. It took me an hour before I found what I was looking for, but there it was—a piece of paper with another number on it. I'd written that number myself on the day of the Falcon's funeral.

There were thirteen digits on the Maltesers box—but the last six of them were all zeroes. Cross those out and you'd be left with seven digits.

A telephone number. And I knew which telephone it rang.

That was when our own telephone rang. The noise of the bell was so sudden, so loud, that I almost dropped the towel. I went into the office and picked it up.

"Nick Diamond?"

The voice was ugly with hatred. I didn't believe a voice could hate that much.

"Gott," I said.

"We have your brother."

That took me by surprise. Herbert? But that was the way Gott worked. He'd snatched Lauren, then me. Why shouldn't he add Herbert to his list?

"If you don't give us what we want," Gott snarled, "he dies."

I didn't have what they wanted, but I wasn't going to say

that. Because suddenly I knew everything. It all made sense. I should have seen it a long, long time before.

"Come to the cemetery," I said. I was talking even before I knew what I was saying. "I'll meet you at the Falcon's grave. Tomorrow at twelve o'clock." I hung up.

I didn't want to get into any arguments.

Then I opened the drawer of Herbert's desk. On the day we had first met the Fat Man, he had given us a card with his telephone number. I called it now, hoping there would be someone in.

"Yes?" It was a flat, neutral voice.

"I want to talk to the Fat Man," I said.

"He's not here."

"It's important I get a message to him."

"Who is this?"

"Nick Diamond."

There was a pause. Then the voice said, "What is the message?"

"I know what the key opens," I said. "And I'm willing to do a deal. Tell the Fat Man to be at Brompton Cemetery tomorrow. At the Falcon's grave at five to twelve exactly. Alone. Have you got that?"

"Yes."

"Good." I hung up on him, too.

After that I made one last call. That was the hardest to make. It cost me five million dollars. But the way I looked at it was like this. The Fat Man had the Maltesers. Gott (and maybe Himmell) had Herbert. And I had the answer. If I'd planned things right, it would all sort itself out the next day at noon.

If I didn't . . . well, we were meeting in a cemetery. At least they wouldn't have to carry me far.

I just hoped it would be a sunny day.

THE SHINING LIGHT

There are only about three or four days in the year when the Brompton Cemetery is more or less empty—and Christmas Day, of course, is one of them. That would suit my plans. Witnesses were one thing I could do without. It was eleven forty-five when I walked up to the Falcon's grave. There was nobody in sight. Fortunately it was another crisp, cloudless day. The sun had no warmth, but it was bright. At least the weather was on my side.

I stood beside the Falcon's grave. The earth was still fresh where they'd buried him, like a sore that hadn't healed. It would take the grass time to grow over it—but where better to find time than in a cemetery? I looked at the memorial, that Victorian telephone booth with the stone falcon perched on top. There's an old saying I thought of. "You can't take it with you." But the Falcon had—or at least, he'd tried his best to. I read the inscription on the memorial. I'd read it before.

THE PATH OF THE JUST IS AS SHINING LIGHT,
THAT SHINETH MORE AND MORE
UNTO THE PERFECT DAY.

The Falcon must have smiled when he had that cut in. I wondered if he was still smiling in his grave.

I heard the gate grind open down at the Fulham Road. That had to be the Fat Man. Sure enough, he appeared a few moments later, wearing a camel-hair coat with real humps. He carried a shooting stick and walked at a jaunty pace, for all the world like a man taking a little exercise before his Christmas lunch.

He saw me standing by the grave, raised the shooting stick, and sauntered over. He was smiling, but only with his lips. His eyes didn't trust me.

"Merry Christmas, Fat Man," I said.

"I hope so," he replied. "And I hope you're not wasting my time, my boy. You should know by now that I don't take kindly to—"

"Have you got the Maltesers?" I cut in.

He nodded. "In my pocket."

"Let me see them."

He took them out but held on to them like he was afraid I was going to grab them.

"Read me the number on the bottom," I said.

He turned the box over: "3521 201 000000." It was the right number. "You say you know what these chocolates meant to the Falcon," he said in a graveyard voice. "You say you want to make a deal. What deal?"

"We'll split the money," I said. "Fifty-fifty."

"Eighty-twenty."

"Sixty-forty."

We were juggling figures. It didn't matter to me. I knew

that once I showed the Fat Man what to do with the Maltesers, I'd be dead. But it was important that he hung on to them. They had to be out in the open.

"Seventy-thirty," the Fat Man said. "It's my last offer."

It was his last offer. There was a movement on the path behind him, and when he turned around there were Gott and Himmell with Herbert between them. It had been a week since I'd last seen him and Herbert had lost weight.

I smiled at him. "Hello, Herbert," I said.

He looked at me reproachfully. "The name is Tim," he muttered.

There are times when my brother really amazes me. I'd been kidnapped, tied up, chased around London, threatened, and half killed. He'd been arrested for murder and kidnapped himself. We were unarmed and surrounded by three psychopathic killers. And he was worried about names. "How are you . . . Tim?" I asked.

"I'm okay," he said. He considered. "Actually I've got a runny nose and—"

"All right," the Fat Man interrupted. "What is this?"

"It's a cemetery," Herbert said.

The Fat Man gritted his teeth.

"Do you know them?" I asked him.

He glanced at Gott and Himmell. "I know them," he said.

"If that little swine is trying to trick us—" Gott began.

"I'm doing what I said I would," I cut in. "I promised I'd lead you to the Maltesers in return for Herbert—I mean—

Tim." I pointed at the Fat Man, who was still holding them. "There they are. And I promised the Fat Man that I'd tell him their secret. If you'll let me, I will."

Nobody said anything. The wind ruffled my hair. I was wearing a warm coat, but my body was far from warm. I just wanted the whole thing to be over.

"Go ahead," Gott said.

"Yes, go ahead," the Fat Man repeated. "And it had better be good."

"All right," I said. "This is how it goes. Henry von Falkenberg was a very careful man, a man who trusted no one. He had five million dollars in diamonds stashed here in England. It was in a safe that had been specially built for him. Even the key to the safe was special. It was designed so that nobody would even know it was a key. Only the Falcon knew. It was the only way he could feel safe himself.

"The Professor built the safe for him—the late Quentin Quisling. I guess we'll never know, but I suppose he built in some sort of device so that Henry von Falkenberg could choose his own combination. That wouldn't have been difficult. The key was a bar code. It could be on a tin of baked beans, a pack of playing cards—a box of Maltesers. The Falcon brought the key with him every time he came to England. If he was searched by the police, he had nothing to fear. Who would suspect that a few black lines on the bottom of a box of candy could open the door to a fortune?

"There was one thing, though. One fail-safe device.

There was a number written on the box. I don't know why. Maybe it appealed to the Falcon's sense of humor. Or maybe it was a clue—a puzzle for his heirs to fight over. But that number was 352-1201 with a few zeroes added to stretch it out. I wrote that number down for my brother on the day of the Falcon's funeral. It's the phone number of this cemetery."

I walked forward to the monument. Nobody spoke, but their eyes followed me like so many gun barrels. I stood on tiptoe and wiped the cuff of my shirt across the eyes of the falcon. As I had guessed, they weren't made of stone. They were glass.

"And where is this ingenious safe?" I asked. "You're looking at it. The Falcon had it designed like a memorial. You see the inscription? The 'shining light' it's referring to is the light beam that opens it. Johnny Naples tried to tell me about that—the sun.

"I won't try to explain to you how a bar code works. I only half understand it myself. But what you're looking at here is the first solar-powered bar-code reader. You've got to hand it to the Professor. He may have been crooked. He may have been a drunk. But he was clever.

"The sunlight goes in through the eyes of the stone falcon. You run the bar code—at a guess—across the open beak. Somewhere inside all this there's a photodetector, a small computer, and an opening device—all solar-powered. If you've got the right bar code, it'll open the safe." I pointed at the Maltesers, still clutched in the Fat Man's hand. "That's the right bar code," I added. "It's as simple as that."

I stopped. Nobody spoke. Only Herbert looked puzzled. He obviously hadn't understood a single word I'd said.

I wasn't exactly sure what was going to happen next, but I'll tell you the general idea. The Fat Man isn't going to share the diamonds with Gott and Himmell. Gott and Himmell clearly have no intention of sharing the diamonds with the Fat Man. But now everybody knows the secret. Herbert and I are forgotten. Nobody cares about us anymore. We slip away to live happily ever after, leaving our three friends to sort themselves out as best they can. That was the general idea. But obviously I'd been talking to the wrong general.

It all happened at once.

Almost casually, the Fat Man had lifted his shooting stick so that the end was pointing at Himmell. At the same time, Gott's hand had slid quietly into his jacket pocket. The two shots were almost simultaneous. Himmell looked down. There was a hole in his chest. The Fat Man lowered his shooting stick. And it was a shooting stick. The smoke was still curling out of the hole at the bottom. He smiled. The smile faded. He frowned. He raised a hand. He'd only just realized that he'd been shot in the neck. This time Gott hadn't used a silencer.

The Fat Man and Himmell slid to the ground together. The Maltesers fell on the grass. The last of the chocolates rolled out.

"Pick it up," Gott said.

I picked up the box. Something was chattering. I was just thinking that it was a bit cold for grasshoppers when I realized what it was. It was Herbert's teeth.

"Give me the box," Gott said.

I gave it to him, then stepped back a pace. Now Herbert and I were standing close together. Gott's gun was out of his jacket. There were too many bandages on his face to be sure, but I think his smile had grown even wider.

"I'm going to enjoy this," he said.

There were two gunshots.

Herbert's hands came up to his stomach. He groaned and lurched forward. "Nick . . ." he whispered. He pitched onto the grave.

I stared at him.

"Get up, Tim," I said.

"But I've been shot."

"No, you haven't."

He held his hands up to his face. There was no blood. He lifted up his shirt and looked underneath. There were no bullet holes. Now he was blushing. "Sorry . . ." he muttered.

Gott had watched this performance with strange, empty eyes. Suddenly he toppled forward. There were two holes in the back of his jacket. He hadn't had time to fire his own gun.

A figure appeared behind him, moving toward us. And that was the biggest surprise of the day.

It was Betty Charlady.

"'Ello, Mr. Nicholas," she gurgled. She was still in her fluffy bedroom slippers, with a forest of artificial flowers on her head. "Wotcha, Mr. Timothy. Blimey! What a turn-up . . . innit!"

"Betty!" Herbert exclaimed. "What are you doing—" But then he plugged his mouth with his thumb, stopping himself in midsentence.

Betty was holding a gun. The gun had just killed Gott.

With a smile, she pulled off her hat and threw it onto the grass. Her wig, with the electric curls, went next. Once more her hand reached up and this time it pulled at the very skin of her face. It stretched, then tore loose, carrying the wrinkles and makeup with it. The gun in her other hand remained steady, but otherwise, in front of our eyes, she was changing.

Betty Charlady was gone. Another woman stood in her place.

"Who is she?" Herbert whispered.

"Beatrice von Falkenberg," I said. "The Falcon's widow. Snape told us that she used to be a great actress. It looks like Mrs. Charlady was one of her performances."

"That's right, boys," Beatrice said.

I took a quick look around the cemetery. The way things were going, I wouldn't have been surprised if the alligator had turned up—perhaps disguised as a hedgehog.

"But . . . but why?" Herbert asked.

"I had to find the diamonds," she said. "My late husband's fortune. When the dwarf gave you the package, I had to get close to you—to find out what you knew. Then I saw your advertisement for a cleaning woman. That gave me the idea."

"And Gott and Himmell were working for you," I said.

"That's very clever of you, Nicholas," she muttered. "How do you know?"

I shrugged. "I told you we were going to the Casablanca Club. You were the only person who knew. But somehow Gott and Himmell managed to turn up just in time to snatch Lauren Bacardi. We led them to her."

Herbert looked at me in astonishment. "That's brilliant," he said.

"There's more. They learned about the Maltesers from Lauren and they told you, Beatrice. That's how you knew what to ask for when I visited you in Hampstead. You were all in it together."

"Until their use ran out," Beatrice said.

"It's incredible," Herbert said.

"Not really," I said. "I almost guessed when I visited Beatrice. She knew your real name. She called you Herbert—not Timothy. And she was wearing the same perfume as Betty. Lavender. That was something she forgot to change."

"You're very clever," Beatrice said.

"Maybe. But there's one thing I don't get. Why did you kill Johnny Naples in the first place?"

She shrugged. "It was an accident. Gott and Himmell had tracked him down to the Hotel Splendide. They were going to snatch him, but I went to see him first. I walked in as Betty

Charlady. Nobody looked twice. I wanted to persuade him to share what he'd found with me. I told him I was his only hope. I could keep Gott and Himmell off his back. And I could use them to stay ahead of the Fat Man. But he was greedy. He wouldn't listen. He had a gun. There was a fight. Like I say, it was an accident." She sighed. "There can't be any more accidents. You two can't leave the cemetery. No witnesses." For a moment she slipped back into her Betty Charlady voice. "Cheerio, then, Mr. Nicholas. Ta, ta, Mr. 'erbert."

She lifted the gun.

"Oh no!" Herbert whimpered.

"I don't think so, Beatrice," I said.

She looked beyond me and her face jerked back like she'd been slapped. But then she lowered the gun and laughed. Suddenly the cemetery was full of uniformed policemen. They were springing up everywhere—out of the long grass and from behind the gravestones. At their head, running to be the first ones to reach us, were Snape and Boyle.

"Well . . . that's a lucky coincidence," Herbert said.

"What do you mean—coincidence?" I said. "I called Snape last night. I told him everything." Herbert's mouth fell open. "Well, I wasn't going to come here alone."

By this time Boyle had reached Beatrice von Falkenberg. She stretched out her hands elegantly for the cuffs, but he threw himself at her anyway—a flying tackle that sent her crashing to the ground.

"You could have come out sooner, Chief Inspector," I said as Snape arrived. "We were nearly killed."

"That's true, laddie," Snape agreed. "But . . . well, it was Boyle. He wanted to see what would happen. He asked me to hold back. And as it's Christmas . . ."

The policemen began to clear away bodies. Snape leaned down and picked up the Maltesers box.

"Now let's see about this," he said.

The three of us gathered around the memorial. The stone falcon waited, its wings spread, its beak open, its glass eyes blinking in the sun. Carefully, Snape tore off the bar code. He threw the rest of the box away. Then he laid the strip faceup in the falcon's beak and pulled it through.

Behind the eyes, inside the falcon's head, a lens focused the sun's beams onto the bar code. The white stripes reflected some of them back onto a photodetector hidden inside the falcon's body. We heard the click as a connection was made. There was a soft hum. A solar-powered generator had sprung to life. It activated a motor. There was another click and the entire front of the memorial—along with the inscription—swung open to reveal a solid metal container.

And that was the last surprise of the day. There was to be no Christmas bonus for Snape, no reward for us. Because there weren't any diamonds. There wasn't even a lump of coal. The container was empty. We were looking at five million dollars' worth of nothing.

THE FALCON'S MALTESER

"But, Nicholas, I still don't understand."

"I've gone through it all twice, Herbert."

"Well, if you wrote it all down . . . That might help."

"Maybe I will."

It was the second day of the New Year. It didn't feel much different from the old year. It was cold. There wasn't any gas in the apartment. And, as usual, we were down to the last handful of change. We'd had a great Christmas, Herbert and me. Two frozen turkey croquettes and the Queen's speech— only we'd missed the Queen's speech. Mum and Dad had sent us a card and a couple of presents, but they hadn't cheered us up. The card showed two koalas in a Christmas tree. The presents were a boomerang for me and a hat with corks for Herbert.

I threw the boomerang away. It came back.

There were still a couple of weeks until school began and I'd have liked to have gone skiing. A lot of the guys in my class had made it to Switzerland or Austria or wherever and they'd be full of it when they got back. It didn't seem fair. After all I'd been through I couldn't even afford the bus fare to the travel agent.

And then the parcel came. Special delivery. From the South of France. It was addressed to me.

I think I knew who it was from before I opened it. There was only one reason I could think of why the Falcon's safe had been empty. I hadn't mentioned it to Snape or Boyle. I hadn't even mentioned it to Herbert.

"What is it?" he asked.

"I don't know."

"Well, open it."

I opened it. Inside the brown wrapping paper there was a carton about the same shape and size as a film box. It was filled with tissue paper, but nestling in the center was a round ball of milk chocolate . . .

"A Malteser!" Herbert said. The color walked out of his face. Herbert didn't much like chocolates anymore. And he hated Maltesers.

There was a card attached to the box. The message was short and not so sweet. It was written in a flowing, looping hand.

No hard feelings?
L.B.

No hard feelings? I wasn't so sure. Lauren had sold me the sob story of her life—and okay, she hadn't had the breaks—but then she'd double-crossed me. All along she'd known more than she'd let on. Maybe she'd worked it out for herself or maybe Johnny Naples had told her. But she'd known about the cemetery and she'd known about the Falcon's memorial. I'd given her the last piece of the puzzle when I told her about the bar code. And that day, in the office of the *Fulham Express,* she'd made up her mind to steal the diamonds. She'd accidentally left the Maltesers upstairs. And when she'd gone up to get them, she'd made a simple copy of the key: a photocopy.

She'd never gone into Fulham Broadway Station—at least, not down to the trains. The moment I'd left, she'd doubled back to the cemetery. Perhaps she'd overtaken me in a taxi. The sun had been shining that day. She'd slid her photocopy through the falcon's beak. And the diamonds had been hers.

I reached down and squeezed the Malteser between my finger and thumb. I was angry. I wanted to see it shatter. But it wouldn't. There was something hard in the center.

"Herbert . . ." I said.

He looked. The chocolate had squashed. It wasn't a Malteser at all. There was something sparkling inside. "What is it?" he asked.

"What does it look like?" I said.

The last of the chocolate had crumbled away. I was left holding a diamond the size of a peanut. What would it be worth? Ten thousand dollars? Twenty thousand? Certainly not peanuts.

So we would go skiing after all. And Herbert would break

his leg as he got onto the plane and we'd blow all the money we got from the diamond before we'd even gotten around to paying the gas bill. But what did I care? It was the New Year and we'd come out of it all alive, and although diamonds may be forever, you've got to grab every good minute and enjoy it while it's there.

Turn the page for a preview of

Public Enemy Number Two

a Diamond Brothers Mystery

FRENCH DICTATION

I didn't like Peregrine Palis from the start. It's a strange thing about French teachers. From my experience they all have either dandruff, bad breath, or silly names. Well, Mr. Palis had all three, and when you add to that the fact that he was on the short side, with a potbelly, a hearing aid, and hair on his neck, you'll agree that he'd never win a Mr. Universe contest . . . or a *Combat Monsieur Univers* as he might say.

He'd only been teaching at the school for three months— if you can call his brand of bullying and sarcasm teaching. Personally I've learned more from a stick of French bread. I remember the first day he strutted into the classroom. He never walked. He moved his legs like he'd forgotten they were attached to his waist. His feet came first, with the rest of his body trying to catch up. Anyway, he wrote his name on the blackboard—just the last bit.

"My name is Palis," he said. "Pronounced 'pallee.' P-A-L-I-S."

We all knew at once that we'd gotten a bad one. He hadn't been in the place thirty seconds and already he'd written his name, pronounced it, and spelled it out. The next thing he'd be having it embroidered on our uniforms. From that moment on, things got steadily worse. He'd treat the smallest mistake like a personal insult. If you spelled something wrong, he'd make you write it out fifty times. If you mispronounced a word, he'd say you were torturing the language. Then he'd torture you. Twisted ears were his specialty. What can I say? French genders were a nightmare. French tenses have never been more tense. After a few months of Mr. Palis, I couldn't even look at French doors without breaking into tears.

Things came to a head as far as I was concerned one Tuesday afternoon in the summer term. We were being given dictation and I leaned over and whispered something to a friend. It wasn't anything very witty. I just wanted to know if to give a French dictation you really had to be a French dictator. The trouble was, the friend laughed. Worse still, Mr. Palis heard him. His head snapped around so fast that his hearing aid nearly fell out. And somehow his eyes fell on me.

"Yes, Simple?" he said.

"I'm sorry, sir?" I asked with an innocent smile.

"Is there something I should know about? Something to give us all a good laugh?" By now he had strutted forward and my left ear was firmly wedged between his thumb and finger. "And what is the French for 'to laugh'?"

"I don't know, sir." I winced.

"It is *rire*. An irregular verb. *Je ris*, *tu ris*, *il rit* . . . I think you had better stay behind after school, Simple. And since you seem to like to laugh so much, you can write out for me the infinitive, participles, present indicative, past historic,

future, and present subjunctive tenses of *rire*. Is that understood?"

"But, sir . . ."

"Are you arguing?"

"No, sir."

Nobody argued with Mr. Palis. Not unless you wanted to
spend the rest of the day writing out the infinitive, participles,
and all the restiples of the French verb *argumenter.*

So that was how I found myself on a sunny afternoon sitting in an empty classroom in an empty school struggling with
the complexities of the last verb I felt like using. There was a
clock ticking above the door. By four-fifteen I'd only gotten
as far as the future. It looked as if my own future wasn't going to be that great. Then the door opened and Boyle and
Snape walked in.

They were the last two people I'd expected to see. They
were the last two people I *wanted* to see: Chief Inspector
Snape of Scotland Yard and his very unlovely assistant Boyle.
Snape was a great lump of a man who always looked as if he
was going to burst out of his clothes, like the Incredible Hulk.
He had pink skin and narrow eyes. Put a pig in a suit and you
wouldn't be able to tell the difference until one of them went
oink. Boyle was just like I remembered him: black hair—
permed on his head, growing wild on his chest. Built like a
boxer and I'm not sure if I mean the fighter or the dog. Boyle
loved violence. And he hated me. I was only thirteen years old

and he seemed to have made it his ambition to make sure that I wouldn't reach fourteen.

"Well, well, well," Snape muttered. "It seems we meet again."

"Pinch me," I said. "I must be dreaming."

Boyle's eyes lit up. "I'll pinch you!" He started toward me.

"Not now, Boyle!" Snape snapped.

"But he said—"

"It was a figure of speech."

Boyle scratched his head as he tried to figure it out. Snape sat on a desk and picked up an exercise book. "What's this?" he asked.

"It's French," I said.

"Yeah? Well, it's all Greek to me." He threw it aside and lit a cigarette. "So how are you keeping?" he asked.

"What are you doing here?" I replied. I had a feeling that they hadn't come to inquire about my health. The only inquiries those two ever made were the sort that people were helping them with.

"We came to see you," Snape said.

"Okay. Well, you've seen me now. So if you don't mind . . ." I reached for my book bag.

"Not so fast, laddie. Not so fast." Snape flicked ash into an inkwell. "The fact is, Boyle and me, we were wondering . . . we need your help."

"My help?"

Snape bit his lip. I could see he didn't like asking me. And

I could understand it. I was just a kid and he was a big shot in Scotland Yard. It hurt his professional pride. Boyle leaned against the wall and scowled. He would rather be hurting me.

"Have you heard of Johnny Powers?" Snape asked.

I shook my head. "Should I have?"

"He was in the papers last April. The front page. He'd just been sent down. He got fifteen years."

"That's too bad."

"Sure, especially as he was only fifteen years old." Snape blew out smoke. "The press called him Public Enemy Number One—and for once they were right. Johnny Powers started young . . ."

"How young?"

"He burned down his kindergarten. He committed his first armed robbery when he was eight years old. Got away with four crates of Mars bars and a barrel of Gatorade. By the time he was thirteen he was the leader of one of the most dangerous gangs in London. They were called the Slingshot Kids . . . which was quite a joke as they were using sawed-off shotguns. Johnny Powers was so crooked he even stole the saw."

There was a long silence.

"What's this got to do with me?" I asked.

"We got Powers last year," Snape went on. "Caught him red-handed trying to steal a million dollars' worth of designer clothes. When Johnny went shoplifting, you were lucky if you were left with the shop."

"So you've got him," I said. "What else do you want?"

"We want the man he was going to sell the clothes to." Snape plunged his cigarette into the inkwell. There was a dull hiss . . . but that might have been Boyle. "The Fence," he went on. "The man who buys and distributes all the stolen property in England . . . and in most of Europe, too.

"You see, Nick, crime is big business. Robberies, burglaries, hijacks, heists . . . every year a mountain of stuff goes missing. Silver candlesticks. Scotch whiskey. Japanese stereos. You name it, somebody's stolen it. And recently we've become aware that one man has set up an operation, a fantastic network to handle it—buying and selling."

"You mean . . . like a shopkeeper?"

"That's just it. He could be a shopkeeper. He could be a banker. He could be anyone. He doesn't get his hands dirty himself, but he's got links with every gang this side of the Atlantic. If we could get our hands on him, it would be a disaster for the underworld. And think of what he could tell us! But he's an invisible man. We don't know what he looks like. We don't know where he lives. To us he's just the Fence. And we want him."

"We want him," Boyle repeated.

"I think I get the general idea, Boyle," I said. I turned back to Snape. "So why don't you ask this Johnny Powers?" I asked.

Snape lit another cigarette. "We have asked him," he replied. "We offered to cut his sentence in half in return for a name. But Powers is crazy. He refused."

"Honor among thieves," I muttered.

"Forget that," Snape said. "Powers would sell his own grandmother if it suited him. In fact he did sell her. She's now working in an Arabian salt mine. But he wouldn't sell her to a policeman. He hates policemen. He wouldn't tell us anything. On the other hand, he might just slip the name to someone he knew. Someone he was friendly with . . ."

"What are you getting at?" I asked. I was beginning to feel uneasy.

"Johnny Powers is fifteen," Snape went on. "Too young for prison—but too dangerous for reform school. So he was sent to a special maximum-security center just outside London—Strangeday Hall. It's for young offenders. No one there is over eighteen. But they're all hardened criminals. We want you to go there."

"Wait a minute . . . !" I swallowed. "I'm not a criminal. I'm not even hardened. I'm a softy. I like cuddly toys. I'm—"

"We'll give you a new name," Snape cut in. "A new identity. You'll share a cell with Powers. And as soon as you've found out what we want to know, we'll have you out of there. You'll be back at school before you even know it."

Out of one prison into another, I thought. But even if I could have skipped the whole term, I wouldn't have considered the offer. Snape might call Powers crazy, but that was the craziest thing I'd ever heard.

"Let me get this straight," I said. "You want to lock me up with some underage Al Capone in a maximum-security jail somewhere outside London. I'm to get friendly with him, preferably before I get my throat cut. And I'm to find out who this Fence is so you can arrest him, too."

"That's right." Snape smiled. "So what do you say?"

"Forget it! Absolutely not! You must be out of your mind, Snape! Not for a million bucks!"

"Can I take that as a no?" Snape asked.

I grabbed my bag and stood up. Mr. Palis and his irregular verbs could wait. I just wanted to get out of there. But at the same time Boyle lurched forward, blocking the way to the door. The look on his face could have blocked a drain.

"Let me persuade him, Chief," he said.

"No, Boyle . . ."

"But—"

"He's decided."

Snape swung himself off the desk. Boyle looked like he was going to explode, but he didn't try to stop me as I reached for the door handle.

"Give me a call if you change your mind," Snape muttered.

"Don't wait up for it," I said.

I left the two of them there and walked home. I didn't think I'd hear from them again. I mean, I'd told them what I thought of their crazy idea—and they could always find some other kid. The way I figured it was, they'd just forget about me and go and look for somebody else.

Which just shows you how much I knew.